LIFE IS A JOKE, AND SO IS LARRY!

LIFE IS A JOKE, AND SO IS LARRY!

FROM THE CRITICALLY ACCLAIMED AUTHOR OF
BLOODY DEMOCRACY

MARWAN JULIO KHADAR

PALMETTO
PUBLISHING
Charleston, SC
www.PalmettoPublishing.com

Hardcover: 9798822978492

Paperback: 9798822978508

eBook: 9798822978515

ACKNOWLEDGEMENT

In the literary world, no book stands alone. I owe a great deal to my editors, Ceara Nobles and Parker Hansen, whose keen insight and meticulous attention to detail helped shape this story into its best form. Working with them was not only productive but also a truly enjoyable experience.

And, of course, my heartfelt thanks go to my family, whose love and encouragement fuel my passion for personal growth. Their unwavering support and understanding of how vital writing is to my life empower me to navigate its challenges with confidence and resilience.

TABLE OF CONTENTS

AUTHOR'S NOTE

For as long as I can remember, I've dreamed of being a wr Not for fame, not for recognition, but because storytell has always been the one thing that feels right. Writing isn't j something I do—it's where I find peace, where my though make sense, where the chaos of life fades into the background

My career in healthcare has been rewarding in many ways, but it has never quite matched the rhythm of my true passion. The deepest fulfillment comes when I'm behind the keyboard, letting creativity flow and shaping words into something meaningful. In those moments, I'm not just writing—I'm becoming the person I was always meant to be.

I come from a family much like the one in this book—a home where laughter is both our greatest defense and our favorite pastime. We tease, we joke, and we find humor in the everyday madness of life. In my family, sarcasm is a love language, and humor isn't just a coping mechanism—it's practically genetic. And let's be honest, while this book is absolutely meant to bring

ABOUT THE AUTHOR

Marwan Khadar's journey begins in Kono, Sierra Leone, a region renowned for its rich diamond resources. His early years were spent in Bo and Kenema, where the vibrant culture and resilience of his homeland shaped his outlook on life. Eventually, he moved to Freetown, the bustling capital city, where his love for storytelling first took root.

His academic path began at Berlin Preparatory School, where he didn't just attend—he excelled, graduating at the top of his class. His hunger for knowledge led him to Albert Academy Secondary School, where he earned two proficiency certificates and distinguished himself in English and literature, proving early on that words were his true calling.

Then came the war. In the early 2000s, as Sierra Leone descended into conflict, Marwan was evacuated from Freetown by the U.S. Embassy, finding himself on the East Coast of the United States as a refugee. Those years tested his resilience but also laid the foundation for his writing career. During that time,

XIV — LIFE IS A JOKE, AND SO IS LARRY —

he penned book synopses—sold anonymously to well-known authors—one of which later became a *New York Times* bestseller. He also ventured into comedy ghostwriting, crafting sharp, unforgettable punchlines for comedians, including one who would go on to be featured on Netflix.

Since 2012, Marwan has called Washington home, drawing inspiration from his incredible journey and the many cultures he has encountered along the way. When he isn't weaving stories, he indulges in his favorite guilty pleasure: binge-watching Korean dramas on Netflix. Music is another wellspring of his creativity, and his playlist includes icons like Julio Iglesias, The Weeknd, Michael Jackson, Bob Marley, and 2Pac—a mix as dynamic as his storytelling.

Beyond writing, Marwan is dedicated to giving back. Every week, he volunteers to assist military veterans, helping with tasks like cleaning, laundry, dog walking, and grocery shopping—small gestures that make a big impact. His love for books extends beyond writing; he is a certified book publisher, earning his credentials from the International Association of Professions Career College, where he is also a proud member.

His life and work are guided by one simple truth:

"When life gets too serious, laughter reminds us how to breathe again."

Marwan Julio Khadar

CHAPTER ONE

Mindy climbed the rickety stairs to Larry's attic room, each step creaking in protest. The house was eerily quiet, but Larry's car still sat parked outside—clear evidence her son was definitely home. Her irritation bubbled over.

"Unbelievable," she muttered. She had hoped—prayed, even—that Larry would finally hold down a job. But judging by his continued presence in bed, that dream had flatlined.

She took a deep breath before calling out, "Larry, get out here! Now!"

Reaching his door, she knocked sharply. "Open up, Larry! You're supposed to be at work, not competing in a one-man hibernation contest!"

A reluctant click sounded, and the door creaked open. The instant Mindy stepped inside, she was ambushed by a stench so offensive it might have been classified as a public health hazard.

"Oh, for the love of—what is that smell? Are you breeding skunks in here?" she demanded, pinching her nose. "Open a window before we both pass out! And explain why you're here instead of scrubbing dishes at that restaurant."

Larry lay sprawled across his bed, staring blankly at the ceiling like a man contemplating the mysteries of the universe— or just too lazy to move. He sighed heavily.

"Got fired yesterday, Ma."

Mindy's jaw dropped. "You got fired? It took you four months to land that job, and you lost it in a single day? What, did you start a food fight? Get into a brawl with the dishwasher?"

"Nah," Larry muttered. "That snitch Charles ratted me out for sleeping in my car. Apparently, I dozed off thirty minutes past my lunch break."

Mindy's eye twitched. "You can't be serious." She flailed her arms. "A lunch break is for eating, Larry—not for slipping into a coma in the parking lot!"

"If they wanted me awake, they should've made the job more interesting," Larry mumbled, rolling onto his side.

"Oh, please," Mindy scoffed. "Your life isn't some tragic novel, and even if it were, it wouldn't be worth much. You weren't performing brain surgery—you were washing dishes! Unless you were cleaning the Queen's fine china, I doubt the thrill factor was supposed to be high." She crossed her arms. "The rent is due in two weeks. If you don't pay up this time, you and your imaginary skunk friend are out on the street."

She punctuated her frustration with a door slam so fierce the walls rattled.

Larry listened to her footsteps retreat before muttering, "My imaginary skunk pal will come through for me. He knows all the best shelters."

With a groan, he dragged himself off the bed and trudged to his cramped bathroom. A few splashes of water later, he descended the stairs, each step feeling like a battle against gravity. The boards groaned under his weight, as though even they were tired of supporting him.

Mindy, now slouched on the couch, was engrossed in an old Jerry Springer episode. She barely glanced up as Larry shuffled past.

"Grab some breakfast if you're hungry. Eggs and sausages are ready," she said, eyes still fixed on the TV drama.

"Thanks, Ma, but I'm good," Larry replied, though his stomach protested.

"Suit yourself," she said with a shrug. "Where are you headed? Please tell me it's the employment office—or at least somewhere useful."

"I saw a job ad for Grandpa's Coffee House. Figured I'd apply," Larry said, heading for the door.

Before stepping out, he caught sight of his Uncle Antonio sprawled on the couch, mouth agape, snoring loud enough to set off car alarms.

"Ma, should we wake Uncle Antonio before the neighbors file a noise complaint? He sounds like a mating call for lazy couch dwellers."

Mindy rolled her eyes. "Let him sleep. At least he's got a job, which is more than I can say for some people."

Larry smirked. "Ma, watching security footage all night isn't a job—it's an endurance test. He probably spent eight hours staring at grainy screens, whispering, 'Did that shadow just move? Oh wait, that's my reflection.'"

With that, he opened the door and stepped outside, letting the warm air wash over him as he braced himself for another round of job hunting—or, more accurately, avoiding another lecture from his mother.

It was the kind of day that made you believe in good things— perfect weather, golden sunlight filtering through the leafy canopy overhead, and a soft breeze that stirred the branches just enough to make the world feel alive. The air carried the distant hum of a lawnmower, blended with an occasional dog's bark and the lazy chirping of birds perched on telephone wires.

The houses, each with its own personality, lined the street in neat rows. Some boasted manicured lawns and flower beds brimming with color, while others showcased the telltale signs of childhood—scattered bikes, chalked-up driveways, and echoes of laughter.

Larry strolled down the sidewalk, soaking in the neighborhood's relaxed rhythm. An older couple walked hand in hand, a jogger zipped past—earbuds in, oblivious to the world—and a pack of kids zigzagged down the street on their bikes, reveling in the simple thrill of speed.

As he neared the intersection by the coffee shop, a familiar sight greeted him: Jerry, the self-appointed king of patio people-watching, seated in his usual spot.

"Jerry, how's it going today?" Larry called, flashing his trademark lopsided grin.

Jerry barely looked up, waving him off like a pesky fly.

"Whoa, did you get a haircut?" Larry teased. "You're looking unusually sharp. What's the occasion? Or did you just wake up and decide to respect yourself for once?"

Jerry sighed theatrically. "Yes, I got a haircut. Tell me, are you already out of friends to annoy, or just warming up? Where are you rushing off to—big date at McDonald's?"

Larry clutched his chest in mock offense. "Oh, Jerry, you wound me. I would never take a date to McDonald's. I'd at least spring for Taco Bell. But no, I'm heading to the coffee shop for my daily dose of caffeine and existential disappointment." He tilted his head. "By the way, how much did your barber pay you for letting him practice on your head? Asking for a broke friend—namely me."

Jerry rolled his eyes but leaned forward, intrigued. "Funny you mention money. My nephew's comedian just bailed on a gig. How'd you like to make a quick hundred bucks entertaining a crowd tonight?"

Larry's ears perked up. "Wait… Boot Camp Bar? The Marine joint? A hundred bucks to make a bunch of beer-fueled, battle-hardened jarheads laugh? Sign me up! I've been saving my best Marine-themed jokes for exactly this situation."

Jerry eyed him skeptically. "Just make sure your jokes are decent, kid. That bar will be packed with Marines, and let's just say they don't appreciate lame jokes. If you bomb hard enough, you might be spending that hundred on stitches."

Larry scoffed. "Please. I've got a whole arsenal of Marine-approved material. They won't know what hit 'em! I'll have 'em rolling on the floor with laughter."

Jerry arched an eyebrow. "Right. Just be sure you can still roll yourself out of there afterward." He shook his head. "Tell your mother I said hi—she's probably the only one who finds you funny."

Larry gasped. "Wow, Jerry. That was a low blow. But fine— I'll take it as a challenge. Just wait till those Marines are laughing so hard they spill their beers. I'll be walking out with pockets stuffed with tip money."

Jerry smirked. "That's what I'm worried about. Try not to end up in the brig, alright? I don't feel like coming down there to bail you out."

Larry gave a mock salute. "Aye, aye, Captain. I'll behave. Maybe I'll even take notes on spit-shining my boots while I'm there."

Jerry waved him off. "Get outta here, ya wise-crackin' punk."

With a grin plastered on his face, Larry strode toward the coffee shop, already mentally rehearsing his set.

The moment he stepped inside, he was hit with a welcome burst of cool air, a sharp contrast to the warmth outside. A departing customer held the door open for him, and he gave a quick nod of thanks before stepping in. The familiar ding of the doorbell rang out as he took in the scene.

The place buzzed with a symphony of sounds—the steady hum of conversations, the rhythmic clatter of ceramic mugs being set down, and the occasional whir of the espresso machine preparing yet another caffeine fix. The rich aroma of freshly brewed coffee mingled with the sugary sweetness of pastries, making Larry's stomach grumble in regret. Maybe skipping breakfast had been a bad idea.

His gaze wandered around the room, landing on the spot where he had once spent countless hours hunched over books, drowning in legal jargon, preparing for the bar exam. Those grueling days had led to repeated failures, crushing his aspirations of becoming a lawyer—and, for a while, his very sense of purpose.

Among the many patrons typing away was Joshua, Larry's old college buddy—the guy who had passed the bar exam on his first try and never let anyone forget it.

Their eyes met across the room, and Joshua's expression shifted from mild surprise to amused curiosity. "Well, well, look who it is. Larry, what brings you here today? I haven't seen you here since… well, let's not reopen old wounds."

Larry strolled over, extending a firm handshake. "How's life defending corporate crooks and ethically questionable billionaires?"

Joshua smirked, leaning back in his chair. "It pays the bills. By the way, how come you didn't show up at Jessica's wedding? Everyone from Wilby High was there—except you."

Larry furrowed his brow. "Jessica? Who'd she marry again?"

Joshua gave him a knowing look. "Todd. Come on, man. Don't tell me that name doesn't still sting a little." He leaned in slightly. "But seriously, are you still clinging to that high school heartbreak? It's been, what, twenty years? You gotta move on, my guy. Let's be real—back then, Todd was the golden boy. Star athlete, prom king, the guy every girl wanted. And you? You were the awkward, lanky kid cracking jokes to distract from the fact that puberty hit you like a slow-moving train."

Larry huffed. "Gee, thanks, Josh. Really needed that nostalgic punch to the gut."

Before Joshua could respond, the familiar ding of the coffee shop's door echoed through the space.

Joshua's lips curled into a smirk. "Oh no. Speak of the devil."

Larry turned instinctively, his stomach tightening. And there she was—Jessica, glowing like she had just walked out of a Hallmark movie, lovingly cradled in Todd's impossibly muscular arms.

"Hello, Jessica," Larry said, keeping his cool. "Hi, Todd."

Joshua, ever the smooth talker, extended a hand. "What's up, guys?"

Todd shook his hand and then turned to Larry, his expression warm—but carrying that slight, patronizing tilt that only former high school legends had perfected. "Larry, I ran into your mom earlier. She mentioned you were here applying for a job."

Larry fought the urge to groan. Really, Ma? He straightened his shoulders and shrugged. "Yeah, I'm on an extended break from stand-up. Just looking for something casual to keep me occupied."

Joshua, ever the wingman, jumped in. "Wait, you're still doing stand-up? That's amazing! You must be killing it." His grin was a little too wide—Larry could tell he was trying to boost his confidence in front of Jessica.

Larry nodded, playing along. "Yeah, man."

Jessica's eyebrows arched in genuine interest. "Professionally?"

"Nah," Larry said, flashing a grin. "I just stand on stage for free to help hecklers refine their insults."

Joshua laughed, nudging Larry. "See? Told you he's the best."

Jessica chuckled. "So, will we be seeing you on TV anytime soon?"

Larry barely hesitated before puffing out his chest. "Not yet, but my agent's working hard to get me a bigger platform. Got an appointment on Friday with a producer from *Def Comedy Jam* in New York."

Jessica's eyes widened. "Wait—the real *Def Comedy Jam?*"

Larry smirked. "No, the one they stream exclusively on Temu. Of course, the real one. And next week, I have a meeting with Netflix."

"Wow, that's incredible!" she beamed. "You have to keep us posted."

"Absolutely."

As soon as Jessica and Todd moved away, Joshua turned to Larry with a skeptical squint.

"You were full of it just now, weren't you?"

Larry sighed. "Totally."

"You don't have an agent, do you?"

"Nope."

"And you don't have any interviews lined up with *Def Comedy Jam* or Netflix?"

"Not even in my wildest daydreams."

Joshua snorted, shaking his head as he held up his fist for a bump. Larry met it with his own, grateful for the unwavering support.

"Way to keep your dignity intact, man," Joshua chuckled.

Larry smirked, watching Jessica and Todd from across the room.

If only I could lie my way into a steady job this easily, he thought.

Joshua's phone buzzed, pulling him away for a quick conversation. Larry watched as his friend gathered his laptop and coat, offered a casual farewell, and strolled outside. Through the coffee shop window, Larry tracked Joshua's movements, his stomach tightening as his old college buddy approached a gleaming BMW X5.

The luxury SUV practically sparkled in the sunlight—a stark contrast to Larry's own battered Toyota, so embarrassingly worn-out that he often opted for the bus instead. The smooth purr of Joshua's engine as he pulled away only deepened Larry's unease. He gave a small wave, but inside, envy gnawed at him. It wasn't just the car—it was the unspoken reminder of how far apart their lives had drifted.

Larry sighed and turned back toward the café, glancing at the barista. He had come here intending to ask about a job, but with Todd and Jessica sitting comfortably nearby, the thought of approaching the counter felt... humiliating.

"Not today," he muttered, stuffing his hands into his pockets before stepping out into the warm afternoon.

As he crossed the parking lot, his phone buzzed in his pocket. He pulled it out and answered.

"Hey, this is Larry. Who's calling?"

A gruff but friendly voice came through the line. "Larry, it's Tom. Just got off the phone with Uncle Jerry—he mentioned you might be available for the comedy gig tonight?"

Larry perked up. "Yeah, Tom! I'm really in a tight spot right now. I'd love the opportunity to perform."

"Well, buddy, today's your lucky day. The bar is desperate for a comedian, and guess what? You're my only option. How do you feel about a regular spot? Every Wednesday, Friday, and Saturday?"

Larry blinked. That sounded dangerously close to a real job. "Depends—what's the pay per night?"

"Two hundred bucks for your first act. If you kill it out there, I'll bump it to three hundred. Just a heads-up—it's a one-time trial for now. If the crowd doesn't respond well, I gotta pull the plug. No hard feelings, but I'd rather not see you get booed off stage."

Larry grinned. "Sounds fair. One last thing—this is all cash, right?"

Tom chuckled. "Why? You dodging the IRS?"

"Please. The only deductions I care about are those buy-one-get-one-free pizza deals, not the ones from my paycheck."

Tom laughed. "Now that's the kind of humor we need. Show up at 9 p.m. and give it your best shot."

"Appreciate it, man! I won't let you down."

"Good to hear. See you tonight."

Larry hung up, feeling lighter for the first time in weeks. Maybe—just maybe—things were starting to turn around.

CHAPTER TWO

Tucked away on the outskirts of Norwalk, Connecticut, Boot Camp Bar was an unexpected treasure—a place where military grit met laid-back camaraderie. From the outside, it didn't look like much. The weathered wooden facade and a steel sign with *Boot Camp Bar* stenciled in bold, military-style lettering gave off an unassuming, almost utilitarian vibe. But there was something inviting about it, a quiet magnetism that pulled in both regulars and first-timers alike. A vintage lantern flickered softly above the entrance, as if giving a knowing nod to those stepping inside.

Beyond the door, the bar was alive with character. Dartboards lined one wall for friendly rivalries, a worn-down pool table stood proudly despite its battle scars, and a snug mini booth doubled as a makeshift stage for stand-up hopefuls like Larry. A beloved haunt for military personnel and their families, *Boot Camp Bar* had also carved out a special place in the hearts of local bikers, creating the perfect mix of rough edges and warm spirits.

Larry, a familiar face at the bar, arrived early and settled into a booth with Tom, the co-owner. As more people trickled in, he excused himself and made his way toward the restroom.

Under the harsh glare of fluorescent lights, Larry faced his reflection in the mirror. He straightened his tie, smoothed his shirt, and locked eyes with himself, summoning every ounce of confidence he could muster.

"Alright, you got this," he murmured, pointing at his reflection like a coach hyping up a player before a big game.

He tested out a few expressions—wide-eyed surprise, a sarcastic smirk, an exaggerated frown.

Shaking his head, he muttered, "What's the deal with these bathroom lights? Were they installed by someone who moonlights as a refrigerator designer?" He chuckled at his own joke.

Then, in a tone shift, he stood tall, rolling his shoulders back. "They'll laugh. And if they don't? Fake it. You're great at that. Remember last month? Ten minutes of absolute bombing, but you walked off stage like you just won an award. That's the energy you need tonight."

Taking one last steadying breath, he winked at his reflection. "Time to turn this awkwardness into applause."

With that, he strode out, stepping onto a stage that was waiting for him.

Larry took a second to absorb the scene. Sure, he'd been here before—but never in the spotlight, never with all eyes locked on him like this.

The air carried a distinct blend of beer, worn leather, and just a hint of salt from the nearby shore, filling the space with an oddly nostalgic charm.

The decor had its own brand of rugged appeal—frayed American flags draped along the walls, slightly crooked military unit photos whispering stories of camaraderie and service. A battered jukebox sat in the corner, waiting for its moment of relevance, while neon beer signs flickered with stubborn determination, as if they, too, had seen a few battles.

The crowd was exactly what he expected—Marines and bikers, their helmets and leather jackets scattered across tables. These were men who had seen it all, lived through it all, and weren't easily impressed. They had traded their crisp military uniforms for faded T-shirts, jeans, and the occasional camo jacket, but their presence carried the same intensity. Some sat back with arms crossed, silently daring Larry to amuse them, while others leaned forward, beers in hand, already grinning in anticipation.

The chatter was loud and animated—deep voices booming, inside jokes flying across tables, and the occasional *"Let's see what you got!"* ringing from the back. The atmosphere crackled with energy, a mix of battle-hardened toughness and an eagerness for a good laugh.

Larry grabbed the mic, let the moment stretch, then smirked.

"Wow, a room full of Marines. It's an honor to be here tonight—mostly because I know that if this set bombs, at least I'm in a room full of professionals who know how to handle a casualty situation."

The room erupted. Laughter rolled through the crowd, glasses clinked, and Tom, standing near the bar, shot Larry a thumbs-up.

Encouraged, Larry grinned. "To be honest, I was a little nervous about performing. Then I reminded myself—what's the worst that could happen? A standing ovation? Or just getting ordered to leave?"

From the back, a drunken Marine hollered, *"Hey, get out of here now! You suck!"*

The room tensed for half a second.

Larry met the heckler's gaze, his grin never faltering. He had been waiting for this.

"A Marine heckling me? Now, that's a man who loves running into danger. Bold move, my friend."

The audience burst into laughter.

Leaning against the mic stand, Larry let the moment settle before delivering his comeback. "Look, I know I'm not the greatest, but at least I don't have to do push-ups every time I bomb a joke. My mom thinks I'm funny, and I trust her judgment a little more than someone who believes camouflage works in a bar. But it's cool, Marine. If I'm not your cup of tea, just chalk me up as another thing the government overpaid for."

The crowd erupted in cheers, whistles echoing through the room.

From the back, Tom nodded approvingly. *That's my guy.*

Larry's eyes landed on an audience member in a striking red jacket—a bold throwback to Michael Jackson's *Thriller* era. He smirked.

"Well, well, check out *Thriller* over here! I had no idea the Marines had a dance-battle division. What's the strategy—moonwalk into combat? Intimidate the enemy with synchronized moves?"

Laughter rippled through the audience, fueling Larry's energy.

"Honestly, if we ever get a zombie apocalypse, I'm sticking with you. That jacket screams, *'I've got the moves and the nerve to survive.'* You'd be taking down zombies with a perfectly timed spin and a solid *hee-hee*."

From the bar, a female Marine called out, her voice playful. "How about my uniform? Skanky enough for you?"

Larry didn't miss a beat. "Skanky? Nah. That uniform doesn't say, *'Drop and give me digits.'* It says, *'Drop and give me twenty.'* It's not skanky—it's legendary. It's the *Beyoncé* of outfits. Flawless. Powerful. Untouchable."

A major in full uniform, seated near the front, gave an approving nod. "Well played."

Larry's tone softened as he addressed the crowd, sincerity replacing sarcasm.

"Before I wrap this up and slink off with my dignity in pieces, I just want to say thank you."

The room quieted, all eyes on him.

"You all put your lives on the line to protect our freedom, and here I am repaying you with bad jokes. Feels like a fair trade, right? You risk everything, and I risk bombing on stage. And let's be real—if you wanted to take me out, I know you wouldn't miss. Your courage, your dedication—it's something else. Me? I lose my mind if the Wi-Fi goes out for five minutes. You're out there dodging bullets, and I'm over here dodging calls from my mom asking for rent."

A few chuckles broke the solemn moment.

"Yeah, I still live with my mom. It's not a big deal… unless you ask her. Whenever someone visits, she's like, *'Oh, this is my 35-year-old son. He's a comedian. That's why he still lives here.'* Like I'm some rare breed of unemployed."

The crowd chuckled as Larry continued, "Living with her is a trip, though. Just the other day, she was making dinner and asked, *'You want meatloaf or lasagna?'* I said, *'Surprise me.'* She goes, *'Surprise you? Okay, I'm not cooking either.'*"

The audience roared with laughter.

"But hey, it's not all bad—free food, free laundry, and a daily roast session. She'll see me watching Netflix at two in the afternoon and be like, *'Wow, the comedy world must be paying off.'* Thanks, Mom. Guess I'll add *professionally roasted* to my resume."

Larry smirked and leaned into the mic. "Alright, that's a wrap, comrades. You've been amazing."

The room erupted into applause as he took a theatrical bow, sealing the night with a wink and a grin.

Tom's grin stretched wide as Larry made his way to the bar, the adrenaline from his set still buzzing in his veins. Without hesitation, Tom pulled him into a bear hug—the kind that said, *You did good, kid.* It was clear that Larry's success on stage felt like a win for both of them.

"Richie!" Tom called out, waving to the bartender. "Pour a shot for our newest recruit."

Richie, always ready to celebrate a victory, slid a glass of amber liquid across the counter with a knowing smile.

With a firm slap on Larry's back, Tom steered him toward a dimly lit corner table, where a lone figure leaned back in her chair, exuding the effortless cool of an old Western gunslinger. A weathered cowboy hat tilted slightly over her face, shadowing her sharp gaze.

"Take a seat, man," Tom said, motioning toward the empty chair. "Meet my business partner, Lucy."

Larry extended a hand, expecting the usual firm but polite handshake. Instead, he was met with a grip strong enough to rival a Marine's—steady, confident, and unapologetically powerful.

Tom, a grizzled man in his late fifties, leaned back in his chair, his tattered leather jacket bearing the scars of a lifetime of stories.

"Tom thinks highly of you," Lucy said, her voice low and even. "And I've got to say, your performance tonight exceeded my expectations. Are you from around here? You look familiar."

"Nah, I'm from Waterbury. But I visit often with Jerry— Tom's uncle."

Lucy's brows lifted slightly. "Jerry? How do you know him?"

"He and my dad served together in Vietnam," Larry said. "Jerry made it out in one piece. My dad... well, he came back missing a leg."

Tom clapped his hands together, cutting the moment before it got too solemn. "Alright, enough of the heavy stuff. Lucy, you're not gonna believe this—Larry's mom is *that* Mindy from Waterbury."

Larry sighed, already bracing himself.

Lucy's expression shifted as recognition clicked. "No way. You must've gone to high school with my niece, Jessica."

"Jessica Tolbert?" Larry blinked.

Lucy nodded. "Yeah! You were that scrawny kid always cracking jokes, weren't you?"

Larry groaned. "Spent a fortune on therapy trying to forget those years. I was so skinny my friends ran out of nicknames. 'Twig,' 'String Bean,' or my personal favorite—*'Hey, are you okay?'* Dating was impossible. Girls were afraid to hold my hand, worried it might snap off."

Lucy chuckled. "Didn't you once deflate your chemistry teacher's tires? I overheard Jessica telling her mom about it."

"No, that was my *English* teacher, Evelyn Harper."

Tom's laugh rumbled low in his chest. "Evelyn Harper? *That* woman? I worked with her at a restaurant in high school—she was a nightmare."

"See?" Larry gestured. "Even Tom agrees."

Lucy smirked. "And what did she do to deserve the tire treatment?"

Larry leaned in. "She gave me an *F.* But it wasn't the grade that bothered me—it was how she announced it. Imagine sitting next to a girl you like, and there's a tiny chance she might say yes to a date. Then Ms. Harper kills all hope with, *'Well, class, it seems someone wrote something so unique, it's practically a crime against literature.'* And to really drive it home, she circled my grade in the brightest red ink as if framing a masterpiece. Then she asked, *'Larry, did you even read the book?'* Like, of course I did—I just didn't realize there'd be a pop quiz on *understanding* it."

Lucy laughed, shaking her head.

Tom, lighting a cigarette, exhaled a cloud of smoke. "Speaking of disasters, we once had a guy here who thought he was an impressionist. Every voice sounded like a dying goat."

Larry grinned. "Well, I don't do impressions, but if the crowd heckles me, I *can* give a flawless impression of a guy who quits mid-set."

Lucy leaned forward. "Quit on us, and you'll be buying drinks all night. We don't do charity here."

"Relax, I'm way funnier than some guy whose best impression sounds like a dying goat. Trust me, I'll have people laughing so hard they'll buy rounds just to keep the party going. And if not, well… I'll stick around and mop the floors. Gotta earn my keep somehow."

Tom arched an eyebrow. "You just might be cocky enough to pull this off."

Lucy smirked, arms crossed. "Fine, but if any of those Marines or those big, burly regulars laugh so hard they spit out their beers, guess who's cleaning it up?"

Larry tapped his chin, pretending to weigh the stakes. "Duly noted. So, we're working with a set list of dying goat impressions and beer-spewing Marines. Sounds like a solid Wednesday night to me."

Tom and Lucy exchanged a knowing glance before bursting into laughter.

"Listen, kid," Tom said, his voice turning serious, "keep the crowd entertained, or you won't last."

Larry grinned. "No pressure, huh? Well, I only need one shot… unless it's whiskey—then I'll take two."

Lucy leaned forward, adjusting her hat slightly. "You've got guts, Larry. Wednesday. Nine sharp. Don't be late."

"Late? Never." Larry stood, shaking her hand. "And don't worry—if the whole thing tanks, I'll be the first comedian to start heckling *myself* on stage."

Lucy chuckled. "Now *that* I'd pay to see."

Tom clapped a firm hand on Larry's shoulder. "Alright then. Next week, bring your best material… or bring a mop. Either way, we'll see you. And enjoy your Thanksgiving tomorrow."

"You too," Larry called over his shoulder as he approached the door.

Once he was out of earshot, Lucy leaned toward Tom, her eyes narrowing. "He looks familiar. I can't place it, but I swear I've seen him before."

Tom exhaled, shaking his head. "Yeah, he used to come in with Uncle Jerry. Spent a lot of nights drowning heartbreak in whiskey after his girl dumped him. Didn't take it well. Plus, word is he flunked his bar exam three times. Sent him into a real spiral."

Lucy frowned. "Poor guy."

Still riding high from the night, Larry hummed to himself as he drove home—right up until the red and blue glare of police lights flashed in his rearview mirror.

"Oh, come on," he muttered, pulling over. He rolled down the window as the officer approached.

"Evening, sir. Do you know why I stopped you?"

Larry sighed. "If it's about that stop sign, I swear it was giving me mixed signals."

The cop arched an unimpressed brow. "You ran it."

"Okay, but I thought stop signs were suggestions. You know, like flossing or eating kale."

No laugh. Tough crowd.

"License and registration."

Larry fished them out and handed them over. The officer studied his license, then looked more closely at him.

"Larry Bianchi?" The officer's expression shifted. "Wait— you went to Wilby High?"

Larry squinted. "Uh… yeah. Who's asking? Are you a fan of my comedy? Because I just killed it at Boot Camp Bar."

The officer chuckled. "Mike Bernard. We had chemistry together. You sat across from me."

Larry blinked. "Wait—goggles Mike?"

Mike's lips quirked. "Yeah, the same Mike you used to rag on every day."

"Oh, that class. The one that taught me chemistry wasn't my thing."

"I loved it," Mike said. "Aced it, actually."

"Good for you. Meanwhile, I'm out here getting pulled over by Bill Nye for a rolling stop."

Mike shook his head, still chuckling. "Hang tight."

As he returned to his patrol car, Larry muttered, "Dodged a fine for sure."

A moment later, Mike was back, handing Larry his license—and a ticket.

Larry frowned. "What's this? A stern warning?"

"Nope. 150-dollar fine." Mike grinned. "And hey, that includes your alumni discount."

"Mike! Come on—just give me a verbal slap on the wrist."

"Sorry, pal. Consider it karma for all the fun you had at my expense. Drive safe. And happy Thanksgiving."

As Mike strolled back to his cruiser, Larry called out, "I HEARD THAT, MIKE! Petty!"

Larry barely had time to process the ticket before his phone rang.

"Hello, Ma—"

"Larry, stop talking. Go buy some garlic. I ran out."

"Crushed or diced?"

"Does it matter?"

Click.

Ten minutes later, he stood in a Walmart checkout line, holding two bags of garlic. The cashier, clearly exhausted from a long shift, barely looked up.

Larry squinted at her nametag. "Laura or Lawra?"

"Either," she muttered.

"All right, Either. What does garlic say to its friends when they're feeling down?"

She sighed. "What?"

"'Don't worry, I've got the zest for life!'"

The guy behind him groaned. "Move it, garlic guy."

Larry turned to see a mountain of a man towering over him. He whistled. "Buddy, your biceps are bigger than my rent check. You don't have to flex both your arms and your schedule."

The man smirked. "Want me to bench-press you out of the way?"

Larry clutched his garlic. "You could, but then I'd tell everyone Hercules personally escorted me out."

The man cracked a grin. "See you in the parking lot, wise-ass."

Larry took that as his cue to leave.

CHAPTER THREE

Mindy was up before sunrise, meticulously seasoning the turkey with a blend of Italian herbs, her hands moving with the precision of a chef who had done this a thousand times before. By the time Larry dragged himself into the kitchen at nine a.m.—hair disheveled and clinging to a mug of coffee like it was his last lifeline—the counter was already overflowing with ingredients, side dishes, and the chaotic energy that could only mean one thing.

He groaned. "Ma, this doesn't look like a *small* gathering."

Mindy barely glanced up as she stuffed the turkey. "We're Italian, Larry. We don't *do* small."

"Right. So, who exactly is on the guest list?"

Mindy scoffed. "Guest list? It's Thanksgiving, not a wedding."

By noon, the house was alive with the sounds of voices, laughter, and the occasional argument. Guests arrived in waves, as they did every year—but this time, with an unexpected addition.

First through the door was Aunt Maria, arms loaded with a tray of cannoli and a dramatic sigh. "Three hours! *Three hours* in traffic to get here! And for what? To watch Mindy overcook a turkey?"

"It's *stuffed,* not overcooked," Mindy shot back, pulling her sister into a hug.

Next came Cousin Gina, beaming as she held hands with her new fiancé, Stefano. He was *ridiculously* handsome—so much so that Larry had to squint, as if Stefano had just stepped out of a cologne commercial.

Larry leaned toward Mindy. "Where'd she find this guy? A Dolce & Gabbana ad?"

"He's Italian, Larry. Be nice."

Then, Nonna arrived, her sharp eyes scanning the room as she shuffled in with a family friend who had driven her over. The moment she spotted Larry, she zeroed in like a heat-seeking missile.

"Larry! Are you still single?"

"Until death, Nonna."

"Why? You're not ugly. You're not stupid—except for failing the bar exam three times. What's the problem? Whatever happened to Sandra? Did you run her off with your jokes?"

"Happy Thanksgiving to you too, Nonna," Larry said, pressing a kiss to her forehead.

Then came Second Cousin Marco, fresh off a spiritual retreat. Dressed in flowing linen pants, he glided into the room like he had just emerged from a meditation retreat in Bali.

"This year, I'm thankful for mindfulness and connection," he announced. "Also, I don't eat anything with a face."

Uncle Antonio, standing beside the turkey, smirked. "More for us, then."

By five o'clock, the dining table was an impressive patchwork of dishes—alongside the turkey and stuffing sat Aunt Maria's lasagna, Uncle Antonio's risotto, and, inexplicably, a massive platter of prosciutto from Tony the Deli Guy, who had somehow ended up on the guest list.

Tony, ever the storyteller, launched into one of his infamous, never-ending anecdotes as he poured wine. "So, there I was, arguing with this guy about mortadella—"

The table collectively passed the breadbasket in silent agreement to tune him out.

As the meal progressed, the conversations grew louder, the wine flowed freely, and, inevitably, the interrogation of Larry's life choices began.

Nonna, eyes sharp as ever, fixed her gaze on him. "So, you're telling jokes now instead of becoming a lawyer? In *our* family, comedy is a personality trait, not a career."

Larry sighed, taking a long sip of his wine. "Here we go."

"When I first met your grandfather, he had *nothing*—just like you do now. But I married him because he made me laugh. These days, women expect more than jokes. You've got quite a challenge ahead of you."

"Nonna, you tell this story every Thanksgiving. Maybe spice it up this year?"

Stefano sat beside Gina, his posture composed, but his eyes betraying a touch of unease. He was doing his best to blend in, though it wasn't easy under Nonna's watchful gaze. She had been sizing him up all evening, and finally, she leaned forward, her voice rising just enough to command the table's attention.

"So, Stefano, you're from Italy, eh? Must have left a whole line of broken hearts behind."

Stefano smiled politely. "No, Nonna. Gina is the only one for me."

Nonna arched a brow, unimpressed. "Really? A handsome man like you? I'd have thought the women would be lining up."

Gina, sensing the subtle interrogation, shot her grandmother a look. "That's a compliment, right?"

"Of course, it's a compliment," Nonna huffed. "I just hope he's not settling."

Gina's jaw dropped. "Settling? *Nonna, I'm right here.*"

"I'm just saying, a man like Stefano deserves the best. I hope you're treating him well—cooking, cleaning, keeping him happy."

Gina folded her arms. "I have a career, Nonna. I don't just cook and clean."

Nonna tilted her head in mock innocence. "Oh, I see. So, who's teaching poor Stefano how to survive on microwave dinners?"

The table erupted into a mix of stifled chuckles and uncomfortable throat-clearings. Uncle Antonio nearly choked on his wine, while Larry bit his lip, struggling not to laugh. Mindy, ever the peacemaker, pinched the bridge of her nose in silent despair.

Stefano, ever the diplomat, offered a warm smile. "Nonna, Gina is wonderful. She makes me very happy."

For a brief moment, Nonna softened, a small smile playing on her wrinkled lips. "She's lucky to have you. So polite. That's rare these days."

Gina threw up her hands. "Okay, I'm officially done. Who wants more mashed potatoes?"

But Nonna wasn't finished. She turned her sharp gaze toward Larry, her voice laced with pointed curiosity. "And you, Larry. You're still telling jokes to strangers instead of becoming a lawyer? When are you going to grow up and retake the bar exam?"

A hush fell over the table. Mindy shot Larry a silent warning, her eyes pleading with him not to take the bait.

Larry, however, was never one to back down—especially when there was a good punchline at stake. He grinned. "Nonna, I've taken the bar exam so many times, they're thinking of renaming the study guides after me."

Nonna did not look amused. "This isn't a joke, Larry. You have a good brain—when you use it. Why waste it on comedy?"

"Waste? Oh, Nonna, you should *see* my audience. They laugh so hard, tears stream down their faces! And you know who else sheds tears? Those poor souls sitting for the bar exam. Trust me, I've seen it—three times now."

Uncle Antonio chuckled. "Three times, huh? Maybe the wine's gone to your head! With your experience at bars, you should've been a *sommelier* instead of aiming for a courtroom."

The table erupted in laughter, except for Nonna, who simply sipped her wine and shook her head.

"Three times, you say? If you fell off a bicycle three times, you'd get back on and learn to ride properly."

"You're absolutely right. But what if that bike just isn't meant for me? Maybe I'm destined to walk instead… and tell jokes about falling off a bike."

More laughter rippled through the table, even coaxing a reluctant smile from Gina, but Nonna remained unyielding.

"Jokes won't pay your bills, young man. You need a *proper* job."

"My jokes help me skip therapy, so I'd say they're paying off."

"You're impossible," Nonna muttered, though a small smirk betrayed her amusement.

"And you're secretly my biggest fan. Come on, admit it. You'll miss me when I'm starring in my own Netflix special."

Nonna took a sip of her wine. "Only if you dedicate it to me."

Larry grinned. "Consider it done. I'll title it *Nonna Knows Best*."

Laughter filled the room once more. Even Mindy couldn't suppress a chuckle, though she sighed with relief as the conversation lightened. For once, Larry had managed to ease the tension with humor—unlike last year's chaos.

The house, once alive with the vibrant sounds of Thanksgiving, had slipped into a serene calm. Empty wine bottles lay scattered, dirty dishes piled high, and the lingering aroma of turkey and herbs filled the air like a nostalgic afterthought. Mindy had insisted—firmly—that no guest should lift a finger to help with cleanup. She was handling it all.

Meanwhile, Larry lounged on his bed, mindlessly scrolling through his phone while replaying the night's playful banter. A grin spread across his face as he recalled Nonna's sharp remarks and Uncle Antonio's animated, wine-fueled tales. Deep down, he knew Nonna's words came from a place of love—even if she had a point.

A soft knock interrupted his thoughts.

"Come in," Larry called out.

The door creaked open. "Hey, are you still awake?"

Larry sat up. "Barely! Are you here to inform me that I'm officially banned from next year's Thanksgiving?"

"Not tonight," Mindy said with a small smirk. "I just... I want to have a real talk. Mind if I sit?"

Larry moved over, and Mindy settled on the edge of his bed, folding her hands in her lap. The usual rigidness in her expression softened, marked by weariness and genuine concern.

"You held your ground tonight, kid. Nonna played tough, but we all know she has a point."

"She always does. But if I can survive Thanksgiving, I think I can manage anything."

Mindy paused, her gaze steady. "That's what I wanted to talk about—your... survival. Your future."

Larry groaned and flopped back onto his pillow. "Ma, please. I just got the family lecture at dinner."

"This isn't about Nonna or the bar exam. It's about *you*. I see you joking through life, downplaying your struggles, and sometimes I wonder if you're really okay."

"What do you mean? I'm fine, Ma."

"Are you really? Since your dad passed, you've changed. You were so young, barely out of college. I know it hit you hard."

Larry stiffened, the lightness in him fading for a moment. "Yeah, it wasn't exactly a wonderful time."

"It wasn't great for any of us, but you seemed to take it the hardest. You stopped planning for the future, treating everything like it could vanish at any moment."

Larry's gaze turned distant as he wrestled with her words. "Maybe. But what's the point of stressing over the future when it's unpredictable?"

Mindy's voice softened. "Larry, your father would have wanted you to live boldly, not hide away. He loved you and was so proud of how your laughter could light up the darkest of times. I *know* comedy brings you joy, and I *know* you're talented. But you can't just drift through life hoping everything magically aligns."

"I'm not drifting. I'm working on my material. I have gigs lined up—they may be small, but they matter."

Mindy nodded. "That's good. But let me ask you—are you truly giving it your all? Or are you skimming the surface because you're scared?"

Larry frowned. "Scared? Scared of what?"

"Of failure. Of totally committing to comedy only to find out it's not enough. So instead, you stay in your comfort zone, convincing yourself you're making progress without really trying. If comedy is your dream, then treat it like one. Put in the effort. *Fight* for it."

Larry sat in silence, letting her words settle deep within him. "And what if it's *not* my dream?"

"Then stop limping along pretending it is. Figure out what you *really* want and chase it down. Do it earnestly—whether it's comedy, law school, or something completely different. You can't linger in the limbo of 'what ifs.' I'm here today, but tomorrow is never guaranteed. Who will look after you when I'm gone? I'm getting older, Larry. Each step up these stairs feels like a marathon."

They exchanged a light chuckle.

"Ma, you're making me sound like a complete slacker."

"I'm a mother; it's in my job description. But I also see a brilliance in you that you don't even recognize. You need to see it, too."

Larry exhaled. "Okay, okay. I get it. Hustle. No more excuses."

"That's all I'm asking. Now, get some rest. Tomorrow is a new day, and it's time to get serious about it." She paused at the door, glancing back at him. "You have what it takes. Don't shy away from proving that—especially to yourself."

With that, she disappeared down the hall, closing the door gently behind her.

Larry reclined against his pillows, her words echoing in his mind. For the first time, a flicker of determination sparked within him. Maybe it was time to stop drifting and push forward with more intention.

Motivated, he grabbed his phone and began researching what it takes to become a *real* stand-up comedian. With a notepad in hand, he jotted down one crucial step: *He needed bigger opportunities.* That meant finding an agent. From what he gathered, agents sought talent with a strong following and serious potential.

That night, Larry took a leap. He signed up for several social media platforms, including TikTok, realizing that his light would shine brightest if he could attract a larger audience.

Larry's phone buzzed insistently on the nightstand, pulling him from sleep. Groggy, he squinted at the glowing screen and swiped to take the call.

"Hello?" he mumbled, voice thick with sleep.

"Larry! It's Uncle Joe. How's my favorite champ doing?"

"Uncle Joe? What time is it in Rome?"

"Rome? Nah, I just got back last night. Listen, you got a minute? I need to chat about something important—I just spoke with Nonna."

Larry sat up, rubbing the sleep from his eyes. "Oh no… what'd she say *now*? Please tell me she didn't start in on how I'm wasting my life again."

"Relax, kid. Nonna's proud of you—well, *mostly*. She mentioned your big comedy dreams. Told me not to harp on your old lawyer ambitions, so I'll respect that. But I *am* here to help you chase those dreams."

Larry frowned. "*You?* Nonna said you don't even have Wi-Fi."

"Why bother with Wi-Fi when you can borrow your neighbor's? And hey, I was a star on stage back in my day—before the sauce took over. But I'm celebrating *five years* sober now, sharper than ever."

"That's awesome, Uncle Joe. Really. But how does this involve me?"

"Simple: You're moving to Jersey with me. I'll help you hone your comedy, get you real gigs—no more open mics for scraps. Waterbury's where dreams go to die, kid. If you want to shine, you come to Jersey—New York's just an hour away. I talked to Mindy; she said you're interested in barista work. Perfect—my buddy owns a coffee shop and would hire you on the spot. Daytime barista, nighttime stand-up. Plus, my friend's got a stake in the New York Comedy Club—an hour away. I'll drive you there every Saturday till you're back on your feet. And maybe get a new car while you're at it—yours is a heap."

"Uncle, that's a lot. I can't just upend my life. I've got… well, sort of a job, some friends. And Ma. It matters."

"I get it. Success isn't just about delivering punchlines—it's about having a guide. Netflix specials don't just happen. Come here, and I'll have you headlining in no time. Do you have any videos of your performances? A killer clip could be your ticket. You on TikTok? Going viral's the new audition."

"I appreciate your concern, but you're asking me to risk everything for something uncertain."

"Kid, staying home with Cheetos and reruns isn't living— it's crying out for help. Trust me, you've got talent, and Bianchis don't settle for average. Remember how I used to sneak you into bars at fifteen to tell jokes? Don't let that spark go to waste. Mindy believes in you, I believe in you—and deep down, you believe in yourself, too. Just think it over."

"Okay, I'll think about it."

"That's my boy! Now, go brush your teeth. You sound like you've been drinking out of a shoe." Uncle Joe's laughter filled the line.

"Thanks for the pep talk, Uncle Joe."

"Anytime, kid. We'll talk soon!"

Larry lingered on the edge of his twin-sized bed, Uncle Joe's words looping in his head. *If you come here, I promise I'll help you secure headlining gigs in no time. You'll shine like a star!* For the first time, leaving his small hometown felt like a tangible possibility.

With a swirl of nerves and hope, he padded downstairs to find Mindy folding laundry in the kitchen. Her warm, steady presence filled the room, grounding him as he turned over the idea of a new future—one step closer to the bright lights of a comedy stage.

"Ma," Larry began, his voice tight with nerves. "I need to talk to you about something important."

Mindy glanced up from the laundry, her hands pausing mid-fold over a bright pair of socks. She studied him for a moment, her mother's instinct kicking in. "You've got that jittery look, sweetheart. What's going on?"

He took a breath, steadying himself. "I'm thinking about moving to New Jersey. Uncle Joe thinks it's a good move. He says I should go all in on comedy."

Mindy exhaled, shaking her head with a small, knowing smile. "Let me guess—Nonna put him up to this?"

"You guessed right."

A flicker of emotions crossed her face—concern, surprise, and something deeper. A quiet pride beneath it all. "New Jersey, huh? That's a big step. Are you sure?"

Larry nodded, though his heart pounded like a drum. "Yeah, Ma. I've been playing it safe for too long. Just like you said last night—I gotta hustle. I mean, what's the worst that could happen? It's only a few hours' drive back home."

Before she could respond, the landline rang, shattering the tense silence. Mindy reached for the receiver, her expression softening as she recognized the voice on the other end.

"It's Nonna," she said, handing the phone to Larry.

He hesitated before pressing the phone to his ear. "Nonna?"

"Larry! My little star!" Nonna's warm, raspy voice filled the line, brimming with affection. "So, you're thinking about New Jersey, eh?"

Larry blinked. "How did you—"

"News travels fast in this family, *caro mio.* Listen to me: Follow your heart. But wherever you go, you'll always be my grandson. I'll pray for you every day. And don't you dare forget to visit—Greenwich isn't far from New York, you know."

Larry swallowed hard, a lump forming in his throat. Nonna had always been his fiercest critic, but she was also his biggest believer. Even when she nagged, it was because she wanted more for him.

"I know I was tough on you at Thanksgiving," she added, as if reading his thoughts. "But it's only because I care. You have talent, Larry. Don't waste it."

His fingers tightened around the phone. "Thanks, Nonna. That means a lot."

After hanging up, he turned back to his mother. She had been watching him quietly, her eyes filled with something he couldn't quite place—melancholy, maybe, but also love.

"Ma, I know this is a risk," he admitted. "But I have to try. If I don't, I'll always wonder."

Mindy reached across the table, taking his hand in hers. "Larry, you're my son, and I just want you to be happy. If this is what you need to do, then do it. Just promise me you'll call often—and for heaven's sake, eat something besides takeout."

Larry let out a breath, a slow grin breaking across his face. The pep talk from Uncle Joe, Nonna's blessing, and his mother's unwavering support were all he needed. For the first time in a long time, he wasn't just dreaming about a different life— he was standing on the edge of it, ready to take that first step.

The sun settled below the horizon, casting a golden glow through the bar's front windows as Tom wiped down the last of the happy-hour glasses. Business had been good—laughter, clinking glasses, the comforting hum of conversation filling the air. Just as he reached for a fresh towel, his phone buzzed on the counter.

A grin spread across Tom's face as he picked up. "Larry! What's cooking, buddy?"

"Tom, my man! How's everything on your end?" Larry's voice crackled with energy.

"Same old, same old—regulars are happy, beer's flowing. What's up?"

"Well," Larry said, his tone taking on that familiar mischievous edge that always meant something big was coming, "I'm planning a special performance this Saturday—an hour-long set. It's time to make my official social media debut, and I'd love for it to happen at your bar. Think you can help spread the word?"

Tom straightened, his bartender instincts kicking in. "A comedy special just for social media? Larry, do you know what that could mean for my bar? Packed seats, good buzz, and some damn fine exposure. I'm in. What do you need from me?"

"Mainly just some promo—an announcement, maybe a banner, something to get people talking. I know it's short notice, but if we move fast, we can make this huge."

Tom tapped his fingers on the counter, thinking. "Listen, I love the idea, but why rush? Let's push it to next Saturday instead. That way, we can really hype it up, get more eyes on it. Trust me, I'll take care of the promo—social media, flyers, posters, the whole nine yards."

Larry exhaled, considering. "Yeah, you're right. Let's do it next Saturday. Gives me time to fine-tune my material."

"Now you're talking," Tom said, rubbing his chin thoughtfully. "We're going all out. I'll rearrange the space for more seating, make sure the sound setup is flawless, and maybe even mix up a few comedy-themed cocktails.

How does *The Punchline Punch* sound?"

Larry let out a laugh. "Tom, you're a legend. This is gonna be amazing."

"Damn right it is," Tom replied. "Now, go work on those jokes—I'll handle the crowd."

With the countdown officially on, the buzz was building. Next Saturday, the bar would be filled with laughter, energy, and maybe—just maybe—the start of something big for Larry Bianchi.

CHAPTER FOUR

Larry leaned casually against the bar, absentmindedly flipping through his notepad while surveying the crowd. Tonight felt different. The usual sea of familiar faces had been replaced by a wonderfully diverse audience—a rare and refreshing sight in this part of town. He spotted a mix of people from all walks of life—Asians, Blacks, Latinos—all gathered under one roof, drawn together by the universal language of laughter.

The bikers, as always, were a rowdy bunch, their booming laughter rivaling the deep rumble of their Harleys parked just outside. Off to the side, Larry noticed a familiar face—a cop seated near the stage, nursing a beer. It took him a second to place the guy, but then it hit him: Officer O'Malley. The same guy who had slapped him with a speeding ticket a few months back. Their eyes met briefly, and Larry caught the subtle flicker of recognition in the officer's gaze—a mix of curiosity and mild suspicion.

Despite the unpredictable mix of personalities, Larry wasn't fazed. Tonight wasn't just another shot in the dark. Tonight, he was here to own the stage.

Before stepping under the spotlight, he made his way over to Tom. "Hey, think you could record my set? I wanna put it up on social media."

Tom shook his head with a grin. "Kid, put that phone away. See that guy over there?" He gestured toward a cameraman adjusting his equipment near the stage. "I hired him for the night."

Larry let out a surprised chuckle. "Wow. You really went all out."

Tom clapped a hand on his shoulder. "Told you, didn't I? Just take a look around—this is the biggest crowd I've had since I took over this place. They came for a great show, so go give 'em one."

Larry nodded, rolling his shoulders to shake off the last of his nerves. This was it.

Stepping onto the stage, he felt the heat of the spotlight settle on him as the chatter in the room began to fade. He grabbed the mic, let the silence stretch for just a second, then flashed a wide grin.

"Good evening, everyone! First off, a huge thank you to all of you for being here tonight. Looking out at this crowd, I can't help but feel inspired. The mix of people in this room— so much diversity—it's a reminder of what makes this country special. I mean, we've got friends here from all backgrounds— Asian, Black, Hispanic—it's like the cast of the world's most underrated sitcom. And speaking of special guests…"

Larry's eyes landed on O'Malley, and a playful glint sparked in his expression. "Let's all give a warm welcome to Officer O'Malley, sitting right here in the audience!"

The crowd turned, and a ripple of applause followed. O'Malley raised his beer in mock salute, a good-natured smirk tugging at his lips.

"Yeah, yeah, let's show him some love. After all, he's technically sponsoring tonight's show—since he gave me a speeding ticket a few months back."

Laughter rippled through the room, loosening up the energy. Even O'Malley cracked a small smile.

Larry grinned, leaning into the mic. "That ticket, though? It really made me think. I had a revelation that day: my car accelerates from zero to sixty a hell of a lot faster than my career."

The crowd erupted, and just like that, the ice was broken.

"Honestly, O'Malley's a stand-up guy. When he pulled me over, he didn't just slap me with a ticket—he gave me some life advice. He said, 'Son, maybe slow down and take a moment to reflect on your life choices.'" Larry paused for effect, then deadpanned, "That's exactly why I was speeding—I was trying to outrun my regrets!"

The laughter hit in waves, rolling through the room like an incoming tide. Larry felt it—he was in the zone. The night was just starting, and he was ready to take this crowd on a ride they wouldn't forget.

Larry smirked, turning toward a cluster of bikers at the bar. "Now, you guys—you're a tough crowd. You roll in here looking like you just stepped off the set of *Mad Max*, and here I am, in my cozy Target khakis, thinking, 'Man, these guys must have wild, battle-hardened stories.' Meanwhile, the craziest thing I've done is eat gas station sushi. That was my version of living on the edge."

One of the bikers let out a loud whoop. "Don't knock gas station sushi!"

"Oh, trust me, I wouldn't dare," Larry shot back, shaking his head. "But that stuff knocked me out—three whole days, gone! I thought I saw the light at the end of the tunnel… turned out it was just the flickering neon glow of a 7-Eleven sign."

Laughter rolled through the bar, and Larry knew he had them. This was his rhythm, his zone.

"Y'know, they say laughter is the best medicine. Unless, of course, you're in court—then the best medicine is a really good lawyer." He grinned. "But seriously, folks, life's too short not to laugh. Unless you're Officer O'Malley, in which case, life's too short not to write a whole lot of tickets."

O'Malley gave a slow, dramatic sip of his beer before tipping it in Larry's direction, drawing cheers from the crowd. Larry felt the rush, the surge of confidence that only a great set could bring. As he scanned the room, his eyes landed on a Black biker near the back, clad in a striking blue leather jacket, laughing heartily.

Larry, never one to let a good moment pass, grinned. "Hey, my guy in the blue—yeah, you! Gotta say, last week, a Marine came in rocking a jacket just like that, but his was red. I see you came in here with the upgrade! Looking sharp, man."

The biker lifted his beer with a wide grin. "You're funny, bro. Keep it going!"

Larry chuckled. "But real quick—I gotta ask. Why is it that whenever I overhear a Black guy on the phone, it always sounds like the most intense conversation ever? Like, 'Man, I swear on everything, if I see you, it's on sight!' Like… bro, are you threatening the DoorDash guy?"

The entire bar burst into laughter, and the biker in blue shook his head, still grinning. "You don't even know, man!"

"And don't even get me started on *'On my mama!'* The second those words are spoken, somebody out there is rethinking all their life choices. And the best part? Half the time, it's over the pettiest stuff! 'Oh, you took my parking spot? That's it, I'm pulling up!' Bro, come on—it's Costco, not *Fight Club!*"

By now, the bar was alive with laughter, people clapping and nudging each other in agreement.

Larry wiped his forehead dramatically. "And speaking of legendary moments—y'all ever listen to Nephew Tommy on the *Steve Harvey Morning Show*? That man is a straight-up genius when it comes to prank calls. If you haven't heard of him, let me tell you—this guy specializes in pushing people's buttons. I remember one call where he pretended to have a stutter, and—no joke—the guy on the other end had a stutter, too. And you know what that guy said? He goes, 'If I come over to your job and find out you don't really stutter, I'm gonna whoop your ass!'"

The room lost it, roaring with laughter.

"And I had to sit there thinking—how do you *know* you could whoop Nephew Tommy's ass? You've never even met the guy! What if Tommy's a whole MMA champ on the side? What if he's got trophies? It's just one of those moments that makes you stop and wonder."

The crowd howled, the energy electric, and Larry knew he had them right where he wanted them. This was what he lived for.

Sweeping his hand toward the audience, he grinned knowingly. "See? Y'all get it. But here's the real beauty of it— you don't even have to fight. Nope. You just talk with so much conviction that the other guy starts rethinking his whole life. Next thing you know, he's like, 'You know what? I'll just Venmo you fifty bucks and call it a day.'"

The room erupted in laughter, and Larry raised his hands in mock surrender, basking in the moment.

"Now, don't get me wrong—I'm not trying to stir up trouble. I've watched enough YouTube street fights to know I am *not* built for that life. I'm just saying, y'all have the best intimidation game I've ever seen. Teach me your ways, my friends."

A man in the back raised his beer and hollered, "You're all right, Larry! You're all right!"

Larry chuckled. "Look, let's be real—Black folks have this magical way of turning regular moments into full-on Broadway productions. Everything they do has *flavor*. You ever been to a

Black church? That's not just a Sunday service—it's a whole *show*. The choir's hitting high notes like they're auditioning for *The Voice*, the ushers got synchronized moves like a dance crew, and your auntie in the back? She's throwing in ad-libs like she's trying to get a record deal."

Laughter rippled through the audience, heads nodding in agreement.

"And let's be honest—being *quiet*? That's just not in the DNA. You ever tried sneaking into a Black church late? Forget it! The usher will *call you out* right in the middle of the sermon. 'Oh, Sister Johnson! So glad you could *finally* join us! Come on down to the front row!'"

A woman in the front row doubled over, laughing so hard she clutched her stomach.

"And don't even get me started on the pastor. Every sermon is *almost* done. He'll be like, 'I'm about to close,' and *thirty minutes later*, we're *still* talking about Moses. Bruh, Moses already crossed the Red Sea—*let us cross the parking lot!*"

The crowd hollered, clapping and wiping away tears of laughter.

"And listen, if we're talking about Black culture, we *have* to talk about the cookout. That's not just a barbecue—it's a *sacred event*. Show up late, and your cousin's clowning you: 'Oh, you just now getting here? We started at *three*. It's *3:05!*'"

The laughter rolled on.

"And you know every cookout has *rules*. Rule number one: don't touch the potato salad unless *you* made it yourself *or* Aunt Gladys personally vouches for you. Rule number two: if the grill master is wearing sandals *with* socks, *trust the process*. That man has been flipping ribs since the '90s. He *knows* what he's doing."

The audience roared, some clapping their hands in agreement.

"Now, Black parents? Y'all *invented* fear. A Black mom can hit you with *that look* from across the room, and suddenly, you remember *every* bad decision you've ever made. And if she ever says, 'Oh, you want something to cry about?'—nah, I'm good. *I do not want something to cry about.*"

The crowd howled in recognition.

"And Black kids? Man, we *knew better* than to ask for stuff in public. 'Mom, can I get some candy?' She hits you with, 'You got candy money?' And you're just standing there like, 'Ma, I'm *seven!* I don't even have a *wallet!*'"

The laughter swelled, rippling through the room like a wave.

"And let's not forget how *everything* in a Black family turns into a *competition.* You're just trying to relax at the family reunion, and suddenly, Uncle Ray is challenging you to a spades match like it's the championship round. And if you *renege?* That's not just a mistake—that's a *betrayal.*"

The crowd groaned and laughed, some nodding in agreement.

"And Black grandmas? The sweetest, *most* intimidating people on earth. They'll feed you like you just came back from war, then guilt-trip you for not visiting. 'Oh, so you *finally* remember me? What, is it my *birthday* or something?'"

The audience clapped and cheered, their laughter blending into one joyful chorus.

"And let's be real—Black folks don't leave a party *on time*. The event 'ends' at nine, but at midnight, we're *still here*. And when somebody says, 'Alright, I'm heading out,' what they *really* mean is, 'I'll be saying my goodbyes for the next thirty minutes.'"

By now, the room was in full-blown hysterics, heads shaking in recognition.

"But here's what I love about Black culture: it's vibrant, loud, and proud. It turns struggle into strength and rhythm into revolution. Black folks don't just survive—they thrive. Nobody does it quite like y'all."

The crowd erupted in applause, beaming with pride and appreciation.

Larry took a slight bow, a huge grin lighting up his face. For the first time, it wasn't just about the jokes—it was about connection, about celebrating culture through laughter. And in that moment, he knew he was doing exactly what he was meant to do.

Still basking in the laughter from his last punchline, Larry let his eyes roam the crowd, soaking in the room's energy. Near the bar, he spotted a small group of people, including two Asian men. One of them was grinning, shaking his head as he laughed with everyone else.

Larry smirked and pointed straight at him. "Oh, look at my guy over here! What's up, man? Don't worry— I'm an equal-opportunity comedian. You're up next!"

The man chuckled, raising his drink in acknowledgment. "Bring it on!"

Larry grinned. "All right, tell me something—why do Chinese restaurants act like soy sauce is liquid gold? You order an entire family feast, and they hand you one lonely little packet. One! What am I supposed to do with that? Season half a noodle?"

The room filled with laughter, and the man at the bar nodded in exaggerated agreement. "Man, that's real! You gotta beg for extra!"

Larry threw up his hands. "Exactly! Why am I out here negotiating for an extra duck sauce packet like I'm closing a business deal? I just want my dumplings to reach their full potential! I swear, they act like we're about to flip these packets on eBay. 'Psst—hey man, I got that premium soy sauce. Fifty cents a packet, cash only.'"

The audience erupted, laughter rolling through in waves.

"And you know you've reached VIP status when you get your takeout and there's no plastic fork inside. That's when they're basically saying, 'Oh, you got this. We trust you. Welcome to the family.'"

The Asian man wiped a tear of laughter from his eye. "Dude, facts!"

Larry nodded. "Right? And let's talk about those fortune cookies for a second. Who's writing these things? 'You will soon embark on a great journey.' Bro, I'm not looking for enlightenment—I just want to know if my General Tso's chicken is gluten-free!"

The audience howled, clapping and cheering. Larry leaned on the mic stand, shaking his head.

"And can we all agree that ninety percent of the time, those fortunes aren't even fortunes? They're just unsolicited life advice.

'Be patient, success is coming.' Uh, thanks, Confucius, but I was kinda hoping for a winning lottery number or something."

The man at the bar was practically doubled over, slapping the table as he laughed. "Man, you've been in my life, haven't you?"

Larry grinned, soaking in the moment. This wasn't just about jokes—it was about connection. And judging by how the crowd was losing it, he was right where he needed to be.

He paced the stage, smiling as he leaned into the mic.

"And tell me this—why does every Asian restaurant feel like a full-blown family operation? You walk in, and it's like stepping into their home. Uncle's back in the kitchen, throwing down with the woks like he's training for the Culinary Olympics. Auntie's at the register, smiling warmly but low-key running the entire operation. And then there's little Kevin in the corner, completely unfazed by the chaos, just knocking out his calculus homework like it's light work. The whole place is a well-oiled machine."

Laughter rippled through the crowd as Larry shook his head.

"And you know you're in an Asian household when the TV remote is wrapped in plastic. Like, are we watching Netflix or preserving a national treasure? That thing looks like it belongs in a museum display case."

The audience chuckled, nodding in agreement.

"And don't even get me started on Asian grocery stores. You walk in thinking, 'I just need a bag of rice,' and somehow leave with a live crab, some dried squid, and a teapot shaped like a lucky cat. You don't even know how it happened—it just did."

The laughter grew, and Larry leaned in, lowering his voice dramatically.

"Speaking of family—Asian parents? Oh, they do **not** play when it comes to grades. You come home with a B, and suddenly, the whole house goes silent. They look at you like you just brought shame upon the ancestors. 'B? Is that short for Be Better?'"

The crowd roared, heads nodding furiously in recognition.

"And why does every Asian kid have to be a piano prodigy? It's like an unspoken rule! By age six, you're already out here playing Beethoven. You better get it right, too, because if your hands are busy on the piano, you can't argue about bedtime at eight."

The audience howled, and Larry smirked.

"But here's the best part about Asian families—they can argue all day over anything. It doesn't even matter what the topic is. No matter how heated it gets, it always ends the same way: 'Are you hungry? Let's eat.'"

More laughter erupted, and Larry spread his hands wide.

"And let's talk about Asian dads for a second. These men are engineering geniuses, and their secret weapon? Duct tape."

He mimed slapping a piece of tape onto something, shaking his head.

"The car's falling apart? Duct tape. The dining chair's missing a leg? Duct tape. You're having an emotional breakdown? 'Here, just duct tape it together!'"

The crowd exploded with laughter, some wiping away tears.

Larry grinned, letting the moment breathe. He wasn't just cracking jokes—he was painting a picture, holding up a mirror, sharing humor that made people feel seen. Judging by the energy in the room, they recognized themselves in every word.

He leaned into the mic, scanning the crowd knowingly.

"All right, let's talk about Asian aunties at family gatherings—because they are the real stars of the show. These women don't hold back. They'll hit you with a backhanded compliment so smooth, you don't even realize you've been roasted until five minutes later. 'Oh, you've gained a little weight!' And before you can react, they're piling food onto your plate like they're fattening you up for winter. Like, Auntie, what do you want from me?!"

The crowd roared, heads nodding in agreement.

"And if you think Asian family gatherings are wild, let's talk about Asian weddings. Oh my goodness, these aren't just celebrations—they're epic sagas. One table's going off with karaoke, another is deep in a game of high-stakes gambling, and then, in the middle of it all, sweet little Grandma grabs the mic for a toast that somehow lasts twice as long as the actual ceremony."

The audience howled as Larry shook his head.

"And let's be real—at an Asian wedding, the bride and groom aren't even the *main event*. The *aunties*? Oh, they own that spotlight. They're busy competing like it's the Achievement Olympics, throwing out their kids' résumés like playing cards. 'Oh, your son's a doctor? That's nice. *My* daughter is married to a *doctor!*'"

More laughter rippled through the room, people wiping their eyes.

"And the moms? They're not just crying at the wedding—they're *judging*. 'Oh, her dress is beautiful… but it's not as nice as your cousin Linda's.'"

The audience erupted, some clapping in recognition.

"And the dads? Oh, they keep it *simple*. Their wedding toasts are basically *life advice* wrapped in a sentence. 'Work hard, save money, and respect your elders.' Then they sit back, sipping tea like they just cracked the code to world peace."

Larry took a step forward, smirking.

"But let's get to the *real* reason people show up—the *wedding banquet*. Forget those boring plated dinners. In an Asian family, you're not just getting a meal—you're entering a *twelve-course endurance challenge*."

The crowd roared as Larry mimed loosening his belt.

"You start off strong, like, 'Oh yeah, I got this!' Then, by course eight, you're just sitting there, *defeated*, contemplating every life choice that led you to this moment."

The laughter was deafening.

Larry grinned, letting the energy settle before delivering the final punchline.

"But you better pace yourself, because just when you think it's over—boom! Someone's shoving another plate in front of you like, 'Eat more! You're too skinny!'"

The audience erupted once more. This wasn't just comedy—it was *storytelling*, a celebration of culture wrapped in laughter. And judging by the joy in the room, everyone felt *right at home.*

"The in-laws—oh man, they *love* to hand out advice, whether you asked for it or not. 'Oh, you're married now? Time to buy a house. And have kids. And don't forget to take care of your parents. And your uncle. And, while you're at it, your uncle's neighbor's dog!' Like, damn, I just said, *I do*—can I breathe first?"

The audience burst into laughter, some nodding in recognition.

"Let's be real—Asian weddings? Absolute *spectacles.* You might invite *500* guests and actually *know* maybe 50 of them. The whole night, you're just shaking hands, smiling, and whispering to your new spouse, 'Who's that?' 'No idea, but I think they're someone's cousin's neighbor's friend's landlord.'"

Larry paced the stage, miming the awkward nods exchanged at these weddings, and the laughter swelled.

"Asian families don't *need* alarm clocks. No, no, no. You ever try sleeping in? The gentle sound of slippers shuffling at *6 a.m.*—that's the *real* wake-up call. Forget iPhone alarms. If you hear those slippers, your day has *officially* begun."

The audience howled, and Larry kept rolling.

"Let's talk about leftovers. Asian moms? *Masters* of repurposing food. You *think* you're getting a fresh meal, but nope! You open that container, and it's like, 'Here's some delicious curry chicken… with a hint of *last year's* kimchi!' And don't act surprised—the scent has *layers* of history in it."

The crowd erupted, and Larry leaned in, lowering his voice like he was sharing a secret.

"If an Asian auntie *ever* showers you with compliments, *brace yourself.* Because right after that sweet moment, *here it comes*— the backhanded roast. 'Oh, you look so pretty! *Too bad you're still single.*'"

Laughter exploded through the room, people slapping their knees.

"And Asian dads? Oh, they can turn *anything* into a life lesson. You're sitting there, watching TV, minding your business, and suddenly, out of nowhere—'You know, when I was your age, I didn't even *have* a TV!' Like, okay, Dad, but I was just trying to enjoy *Jeopardy*, not get hit with a history lesson."

The audience roared, and Larry shook his head, pretending to be his dad, sitting back in his chair and nodding wisely.

"Oh, and if you're hoping for an *allowance* in an Asian household? Ha! *Good luck.* You want spending money? You better win a math competition or clock in some hours at the family restaurant. 'You want money? *Go sweep something.*'"

The laughter swelled into a full-blown wave, and Larry grinned, soaking it all in. This wasn't just comedy—it was *shared experience*, a celebration of culture wrapped in jokes. And judging by the crowd's reaction, everyone *felt* it, too.

"You ever notice how family back home *always* calls at the *worst* possible time? Like, you're just trying to enjoy dinner, finally about to take that *first bite*, and—*ring ring!*—'Why you no call more often?' Bro, because it's *3 a.m.* where you are, and I'm just trying to eat my *lo mein* in peace!"

The audience erupted, and over at the bar, one man was practically doubled over, laughing so hard he clutched his stomach.

"Man, you've been spying on my life!" he gasped between laughs.

Larry smirked and pointed at him. "Hey, don't worry. You're *not* alone. Every Chinese grandma I've ever met has three settings: *love, guilt trip,* and 'Why you so skinny? *Eat more!*'"

The crowd lost it, clapping and hollering in agreement. Larry held up his hands.

"Here's the thing—Chinese food? That stuff is *magic.* You can stuff yourself full, feel like you might explode, and then, *boom,* an hour later, you're back in the fridge like a raccoon on a mission. I just inhaled *3,000 calories,* and suddenly, my stomach's acting like it's been *betrayed.* What kind of *sorcery* is that? Is it *MSG?* Is it some ancient *black hole physics?* We'll *never* know."

The Asian man at the bar was pounding the table now, laughing so hard he had to wipe his eyes. "That's *too* real!" he shouted.

Larry took a slow sip of water, nodding.

"My guy, you're a *champ* for this. And for the record? Chinese food isn't just a *meal*—it's an *experience*. Forget Michelin stars. Give me some Kung Pao chicken and an extra side of rice, and I'm *set for life*."

As the applause thundered through the room, Larry turned back toward the man at the bar, flashing him an appreciative nod.

"Gotta give it up for you, man. You made this set *way* better."

Still riding the high of the moment, Larry let his gaze sweep across the crowd again, his eyes landing on a man near the front—a Mexican guy who looked like he owned the night. Draped in a bright, colorful poncho, he sipped a margarita like he was on vacation in his own personal paradise. His mouth gleamed with a full set of gold teeth, each one catching the light every time he grinned. His jewelry screamed success—a massive gold chain rested heavily on his chest, its pendant so big it might as well have its own zip code, perfectly matching the oversized watch on his wrist that sparkled with every flick of his hand. Leaning back in his seat, he exuded effortless confidence, like a king holding court at his own fiesta. His energy was infectious, and Larry couldn't resist calling him out.

"Oh man, look at this legend right here! My guy is thriving! Poncho on, margarita in hand—you've already won the night, and the rest of us are just playing catch-up."

The man lit up, flashing a huge grin as he raised his glass. "You're killing it, bro! Keep it going!"

Larry chuckled, nodding. "See, this is why I love my Mexican brothers and sisters. Y'all have the best sense of humor—hands down. But let's be real… sometimes your jokes? Uh, different. Like, I'll be hanging out with my Mexican friends, and they'll drop something that either has me crying laughing or just sitting there like, 'Wait… am I missing something?'"

The audience cracked up, some nudging their friends as Larry shook his head with a grin.

"Like one time, I heard this gem: 'What do you call a guy with no arms and no legs in a pile of leaves? Russell.'"

The room erupted, but Larry widened his eyes, playing up his confusion.

"And my Mexican friend? Losing his mind. Like, this was peak comedy. Meanwhile, I'm just sitting there thinking, 'Is this a cultural thing, or am I just too slow?'"

The man in the poncho was practically wheezing, nodding as he tried to catch his breath. "Facts, bro! FACTS!"

Larry pointed at him, smirking. "See?! Y'all live for these jokes! And let's not forget the classics. Every Mexican family has that joke—the one that gets told at every party, barbecue, and quinceañera. You already know which one I'm talking about—'Why did the tomato turn red? Because it saw the salsa!'"

The crowd roared, a few people clapping and shaking their heads like they'd heard that joke a hundred times before.

Larry grinned. "That's not just a joke—that's a family heirloom. That joke gets passed down through generations. Your grandpa told it, your uncle tells it, and one day, you're gonna be telling it at a party, just like, 'Hey, y'all ever heard this one?'"

The man in the poncho wiped his eyes, still laughing. "Man, you grew up with us or what?!"

Larry spread his arms wide, grinning. "One of my absolute favorite things about Mexican humor is the way y'all roast each other. It's an art form, really. You step into a Mexican barbecue, and before you can even grab a plate, the jokes start flying like sparks off the grill."

"Hey, primo! Why you built like a pinata? All hollow and no candy! It's ruthless. It's relentless. And yet, it's all love."

The man in the poncho was doubled over, wiping tears from his eyes, barely able to catch a breath.

Larry pointed at him with a grin. "And you know what? I respect it. Because no matter how savage the roast, no matter how deep the cut, it always ends the same way: 'Here, have some tacos.' And let's be real—you can't stay mad when there are tacos involved."

The crowd roared, the energy in the room rising to a near fever pitch. Larry took a step back, letting the waves of laughter crash over him before delivering the final punch.

"So, to my Mexican brothers and sisters, gracias. Thank you for proving to the world that life is better when you can laugh at yourself, roast your loved ones, and drown it all in good salsa. Y'all are the real MVPs!"

A thunderous round of applause erupted. The man in the poncho lifted his glass high and shouted, "You killed it, man!"

Larry gave a small, theatrical bow, basking in the glow of shared joy. At that moment, he knew he had tapped into something special—the magic of laughter, connection, and celebrating the quirks that made people who they were.

Adjusting the mic, he strummed a fresh, catchy riff. "Now, let's take a second to appreciate my wonderful Mexican brothers and sisters—and their, let's call them… unique job titles. Because, let's be honest, y'all do some of the wildest, most creative work out there."

The crowd cheered, ready for whatever came next.

The man in the poncho raised his drink, his face glowing with excitement. "We want to hear it, man!"

Larry chuckled, shaking his head as he gestured toward him.

"Oh, you already know what I'm about to say. You meet a Mexican guy, and he'll hit you with, 'Yeah, I mow lawns, fix roofs, paint houses, train dogs, and on weekends, I sing mariachi.' Bro—pick a lane!"

The room exploded with laughter—the kind that comes from deep, undeniable truth.

"And what blows my mind? They're amazing at all of it! You call Juan to fix a leaky pipe, next thing you know, your whole bathroom's been renovated. And just as he's packing up, he casually goes, 'By the way, I made tamales. Want some?' Like, bro, how are you running a construction company and a catering business at the same time?"

The man in the poncho was wiping away tears of laughter. "That's my uncle, man!"

"Exactly! And don't even get me started on the party gigs." Larry grinned, pacing the stage like he was revealing a great mystery. "Every Mexican family has that one cousin—clown by day, DJ by night. You'll see him at noon, making balloon animals for kids. Fast forward to 10 p.m., and he's behind the turntables yelling, '¡Arriba, arriba!'"

The crowd howled, and Larry pressed on.

"And then there's that one guy—the seasonal job master. Summer? He's out pushing a paleta cart. Fall? He's running the pumpkin patch. Winter? Boom—he's Santa at the mall. Like, how does he have more job titles than a CEO on LinkedIn?"

The man in the poncho nearly fell out of his seat, gasping between laughs. "It's true, man! We hustle!"

"That's exactly what I respect! Y'all don't wait for opportunities—you make them. I knew a guy who ran a taco truck, did landscaping on the side, and still taught salsa classes at night. Meanwhile, I'm over here struggling to finish my taxes."

The room erupted, waves of laughter rolling through the crowd. Larry lifted his hands in salute.

"So, here's to the hardest-working people out there. Y'all don't just do the job—you own it. And you make it look effortless. Now, if anyone needs a new roof, a fresh haircut, or a piñata shaped like their ex—just hit up my guy in the poncho. I guarantee he knows someone."

The applause was deafening, the laughter infectious. Larry grinned, knowing he had just turned the truth into comedy gold.

"All right, let's talk about something spicy—crossing the border. Yeah, I'm going there, so just hang in with me! It's all in good fun, I promise."

A ripple of nervous laughter swept through the crowd. Larry flashed a mischievous grin, leaning into the mic.

"You see, Mexicans have taken something technically illegal and turned it into a full-blown sport. Have you ever seen someone scale a fence that fast? It's like watching an Olympic event mixed with a Cirque du Soleil performance. The agility, the precision—it's unreal! I catch myself wondering, 'Is this an escape… or a Nike commercial?'"

The man in the poncho let out a booming laugh, raising his glass. "Exactly, my friend!"

Larry pointed at him. "See? We're on the same wavelength! And you have to respect the sheer creativity. Crossing the border isn't just a journey—it's an episode of *MacGyver* in real life. These folks will take a spare tire and turn it into a raft, rig a leaf blower into a jetpack, and the next thing you know, they're in Texas eating barbecue. Meanwhile, I can't even set up a camping tent without watching a YouTube tutorial!"

The laughter in the room grew louder, shaking the walls. Larry grinned and pressed on.

"Let's talk about those insane hiding techniques. Have y'all heard these stories? People squeezing into car trunks, hiding inside dashboards—you name it. There was one guy who literally curled himself up inside a car seat. Bro looked like he was auditioning for *Transformers*! How does someone even think of that? Meanwhile, I'm over here complaining about legroom on a two-hour flight."

The audience erupted, clapping and cheering, the energy electric. Larry leaned back, soaking in the moment, knowing he had just turned ingenuity into comedy gold.

Even the cop in the back was laughing now, shaking his head as Larry kept rolling with the jokes.

"And what about the sheer creativity when it comes to excuses? You catch someone mid-crossing, and they don't even flinch. 'Oh, officer! Crossing the border? No way! I was just sightseeing! Have you seen that gorgeous cactus over there? Stunning! And wow, I had no idea the Rio Grande was that deep!'"

The man in the poncho nearly fell out of his chair. "Bro, stop! You're killing me!"

Larry chuckled, shaking his head. "But let's be real—you have to respect the hustle. Making that journey takes some serious guts. And once they're here? They're working three jobs, raising five kids, and still managing to send money back home. Meanwhile, I can barely keep up with my emails."

The crowd roared, laughter echoing off the walls. Larry lifted his hands dramatically.

"So, to all my incredible friends who've taken that journey—whether through legal means or with a little extra… creativity—I salute you. You're not just crossing borders; you're breaking records. Somebody give these folks a gold medal because they're out here accomplishing the impossible while I'm over here gasping for air after climbing three flights of stairs."

The room exploded into applause. Larry took a slight bow, his grin stretching from ear to ear.

"All right, let's keep it going before someone builds a wall around me. Who's next?"

As he adjusted his mic, his eyes landed on a man front and center, proudly rocking a bright red *Make America Great Again* hat. Larry couldn't help but smirk.

"Oh, look at this guy. Right up front with the MAGA hat. Bold move, my friend. You're like a biker at a Prius convention— you definitely stand out."

The crowd chuckled as the man tipped his hat with a playful smirk.

"Listen, I respect it. You're wearing that hat like it's bulletproof. And let's be honest—being a Trump supporter in public takes serious nerve. It's like showing up to a vegan barbecue with a full tray of ribs. You *know* you're stirring the pot, and you're thriving on it."

The audience erupted in laughter, and the man shot Larry a thumbs-up. "Keep it coming!" he shouted with enthusiasm.

Larry's grin widened as he leaned into the mic. "Oh, I will! You Trump supporters are a different breed. Your loyalty is on another level. No matter what he says—if Trump wakes up tomorrow and declares the sky is green, y'all would be out there like, 'It's green! The most fabulous shade of green I've ever seen. Frankly, the best green, believe me.'"

Laughter rolled through the crowd, a mix of chuckles and outright cackles. Larry kept the momentum going.

"And y'all sure do love those rallies, huh? Man, when Trump announces a rally, it's like a full-blown family road trip. Three generations pile into a pickup truck like it's the Super Bowl of politics. Grandpa's in the back waving an American flag, Mom's rocking her *Don't Tread on Me* shirt, and little Billy's proudly clutching a *Build the Wall* sign—meanwhile, his babysitter Maria is just there, watching."

Even the guy in the MAGA hat was laughing now, shaking his head with a smirk. Larry pointed at him. "See? Even you know it's true."

His eyes twinkled with mischief as he continued.

"Let's talk about these slogans. *Make America Great Again?* I mean, what's the actual plan? Are we bringing back Blockbuster and MySpace? Because let's be honest—gas prices aren't dipping to 99 cents anytime soon."

The room erupted, a mix of applause and roaring laughter. Larry glanced back at the man in the MAGA hat, who was still grinning.

"But listen—I gotta hand it to y'all. The passion is unmatched. I've seen Trump supporters go all day debating on Facebook. It's impressive. Meanwhile, I can't even last ten minutes trying to remember my Netflix password."

The laughter built again, and Larry leaned in with a mock-serious expression.

"But what really gets me? The optimism. Y'all truly believe in America so much that you think a simple *hat* can fix everything. It's honestly hilarious. Like, if hats had that much power, I'd have been rocking a *Make the Bar Exam Easy Again* cap years ago."

He let the crowd settle for a second before delivering the final punch.

"And the dedication? Unmatched. Y'all would argue with a stop sign if you thought it leaned too far left."

The crowd burst into laughter, and the man in the MAGA hat stood up, cheering. "You're a good one, Larry. You really are!"

Larry offered a slight bow, a smirk playing at the corner of his lips.

"You always know when you're talking to a MAGA supporter— their definition of *fake news* includes every major media outlet, yet they'll trust a blurry meme from *FreedomEaglePatriot. net* without question. MAGA folks have a special talent for turning a casual barbecue into a full-blown political rally. One minute, you're savoring some ribs and a cold beer, and the next, someone's passionately declaring, 'And that's why we need to bring back coal!'"

He shook his head, chuckling. "Ever notice how they love to shout, *'We're taking America back!'* But back from who, exactly? The HOA? It's always amusing how they rail against socialism— right before wheeling out a shopping cart overflowing with Walmart's finest coupon deals. And don't even *think* about suggesting a vegan option at their cookout. MAGA is all about *freedom*—until you put tofu on the grill."

Larry leaned in, voice dropping conspiratorially. "You *know* you're at a MAGA rally when the Wi-Fi password is *BuildTheWall2024,* and the only sites it connects to are Fox News and Breitbart. These folks will argue for hours about election fraud, yet give them a QR code menu at a restaurant, and suddenly it's sorcery. *'What is this witchcraft? Is this part of the liberal agenda?'"*

He sighed dramatically. "I once asked a MAGA supporter why they worship Trump, and they said, *'Because he tells it like it is.'* I said, *'You mean he tweets it like it is?'* And just like that—I was blocked! You *know* Trump has a Twitter obsession when he seems more dedicated to firing off tweets than reading a single briefing memo. Why read when you can rant in all caps? They say he doesn't drink, but his 3 a.m. Twitter meltdowns have the same chaotic energy as someone five tequila shots deep."

Larry paused, then added with a knowing look, "His negotiation style? Oh, it's something else. He starts with an *outrageous* demand, watches it collapse, and then blames everyone else. *'Mexico didn't pay for the wall? Fake news!'*And speaking of that wall—he promised to build it, but the only real wall he constructed was between himself and reality. His hairstyle hasn't changed in decades, which just proves even his *barber* can't talk him into a new idea. They say he never backs down from a fight—unless that fight is with facts. If you ever think you're exaggerating, just remember: Trump once claimed he had the *largest inauguration crowd in history. Period."*

Larry paused to let the chatter and laughter settle.

"I've got a soft spot for Trump, I really do. He's the only guy who doesn't need a diary—his tweets *are* his diary, except the whole world gets a front-row seat. His idea of compromise? Letting someone else talk just long enough for him to interrupt. People say his speeches are unpredictable, but come on— you *know* you're getting 'China,' 'Fake News,' and a brag about something that never actually happened. Sure, they say he made his fortune in real estate, but let's be honest—his real talent is living rent-free in everyone's head."

The man in the MAGA hat chuckled along with the rest of the crowd.

"All in good fun, my friend," Larry said, flashing a grin. "Just remember, I'm a comedian, not a politician. My job is to make people laugh, not start debates. Let's keep the party going before someone decides to launch a campaign sign my way."

Larry's eyes lit up as he zeroed in on a couple near the bar. He pointed at them with a playful grin.

"Oh, look at this adorable duo! Y'all have that 'we met at a family reunion and decided it wasn't *that* weird' kind of vibe."

The room erupted in laughter, and the man lifted his drink, shaking his head. "Don't start with me, Larry!"

Larry chuckled, holding up his hands in mock surrender. "Hey, I'm just saying—you two definitely look like you locked eyes over a funnel cake at the county fair. Am I close?"

The woman laughed, shaking her head. "Close enough!"

"Knew it!" Larry smirked. "And let me guess—y'all had a wedding registry at Bass Pro Shops, right? *'Honey, should we go with the camouflage toaster or the personalized fishing poles?'*"

The audience roared with laughter.

"Southern marriages hit different," Larry continued. "Y'all argue about the wildest things. It's never, *'Why didn't you take out the trash?'* It's, *'Why'd you let the dog drink my Bud Light again?'*"

The couple doubled over, and Larry wasn't about to let up.

"And don't even get me started on public fights. Southern couples will go *at it* in Walmart over which brand of BBQ sauce to get, and five minutes later—boom! They're holding hands in the checkout line like nothing ever happened. That's *real* love."

The man raised his hand in surrender. "Larry, you know way too much about us!"

Larry grinned. "It's a gift, my friend. But let's talk about your date nights. Nobody does romance like Southern couples. It's never, *'Let's go to a fancy restaurant.'* Nah, it's, *'Babe, you wanna hit the Waffle House after the tractor pull?'* And somehow, that's a *five-star* evening."

The crowd roared, and Larry pointed at the man.

"And you, my guy—I *know* you're the romantic type. You probably proposed with a ring you won out of a claw machine, didn't you?"

The man laughed, shaking his head. "It was *Cracker Barrel,* thank you very much!"

Larry doubled over, laughing. "See, that's *even better!* Cracker Barrel proposals— *'Baby, I love you more than biscuits and gravy. Will you be my forever hunting partner?'*"

The woman wiped tears of laughter from her eyes, and Larry gave them a playful bow.

"But honestly, I respect y'all. Southern marriages last forever. Why? Because y'all know how to keep it simple. It's like, *'As long as we've got sweet tea, a grill, and a truck that runs, we're happy.'* And I think that's beautiful."

The audience erupted into applause, the couple clapping along as they laughed.

"Y'all are great. Just don't go letting the dog drink your beer tonight, all right?"

Larry turned his attention back to the crowd.

He scanned the room, his eyes twinkling with mischief. "Looking out at all of you, I see a lot of folks who are either *damaged goods*—by which I mean divorced—or just didn't quite fit into someone else's perfect little box. And you know what? That's okay! In fact, let's *celebrate* that! Because if you're single, congratulations—you *might* just have a few extra years of peace and freedom compared to your married friends."

Half the audience raised their hands, laughing in agreement.

Larry leaned in, lowering his voice like he was about to reveal a great conspiracy. "Alright, hear me out. Some say marriage is one of history's greatest social constructs. But me? I think it was created as a form of population control."

A murmur of curiosity swept through the room.

"Think about it. Back in ancient times, before organized religion took over, people supposedly lived for *centuries*. That's a *long* time to be collecting government benefits, right? So some very clever minds thought, *'Wait a second, we can't afford all these old folks hanging around forever. What if we make life just stressful enough to shave off a few decades?'* And boom— *marriage* was born."

The crowd erupted into laughter.

"Then they threw in religion to *seal the deal*— *'God wants you to get married!'* they said. So now, people tie the knot thinking it's divine destiny, when really, it's just an expedited path to gray hair, high blood pressure, and an early grave."

He smirked, pacing the stage. "Now, in the Middle East, they put a different spin on it. Some laws allow men to have up to *four* wives. Sounds like a sweet deal, right? But let's be real—it's just a more *sugar-coated* version of the same poison pill. Whether it's one wife or four, the outcome's the same— stress, drama, and an early check-out."

The audience howled.

"But here's where it gets really interesting," Larry continued. "Western society figured out a *faster* way to send men to an early grave—monogamy. See, in polygamy, if a guy has multiple wives, they're usually too busy arguing with *each other* to put all their energy into nagging *him*. That means *less* stress, which means—get this—he actually has a *better* chance of making it to old age. Maybe even an extra *five to ten years!*"

He shrugged dramatically. "So fellas, if you want to *extend* your lifespan, your best bet might just be to pack your bags, move to the Middle East, and convert to Islam. *It's science!*"

The crowd *erupted* into laughter, tables rattling as people banged their hands against them. A group of women shot up from their seats, playfully giving Larry *thumbs down,* clearly unimpressed by the mention of polygamy.

Larry grinned, holding up his hands in defense. "Alright, alright, I get it! Marriage isn't *all* bad—it's just a never-ending group project where one of you thinks they're carrying all the weight while the other is happily 'supervising.'"

The laughter rolled on as he continued. "You know you've reached *peak* married life when 'date night' means curling up on the couch together, each of you scrolling on your phones in complete silence—but somehow, it *still* counts as quality time. They say marriage is all about sharing, and that's true… *until* it comes to fries. Then, suddenly, it's an all-out war. *'Why didn't you order your own?!'"*

The women in the audience nodded knowingly, nudging their husbands as Larry kept going.

"Before you say 'I do,' it's all romance—flowers, candlelit dinners, the works. After marriage? It's a *full-blown* battle over the right way to load the dishwasher. And apparently, that's a hill some people are willing to *die* on."

He paced the stage, smirking. "Once you're married, your spouse takes on *multiple* roles—partner, best friend, personal reminder system. *'Hey, don't forget to call your mom.' 'Hey, take out the trash.' 'Hey, don't forget to breathe.'* My buddy's wife always complains that he doesn't listen. He swears that's not true—he just has *selective* hearing. She says, *'Clean the garage,'* and it's like static on the radio. But *'There's cake in the fridge'?* Suddenly, he's got superhero-level clarity."

The audience roared with laughter.

"My uncle once told me that marriage is all about *compromise.* Just last week, he and my aunt reached a *solid* middle ground—she got to watch her favorite show, and he got to discreetly Google *'how to fake a power outage'* without getting caught."

Larry paused, then grinned. "But at the end of the day, the best part of marriage? Having someone who loves and supports you, through thick and thin. The *not-so-great* part? Sharing a bed with a *human tornado* who turns the blankets into their own personal *capture-the-flag* game."

The room exploded with laughter, couples nudging each other in mock accusation as Larry took a satisfied bow.

"Marriage is basically signing up to argue with the same person for the rest of your life. But hey, at least you don't have to go through the hassle of *disappointing new people*—it's just one lifelong commitment to letting this person down. They say marriage is a partnership, but why does it feel like my spouse owns *90%* of the company, and I'm just the unpaid intern fetching coffee and saying, *'Great idea, honey!'?*"

He took a sip of water, shaking his head.

"My mother always said marriage teaches *patience*. And she's right—like the patience of waiting for your spouse to finish their show so you can *finally* start yours. *Three years later.*"

The audience cracked up.

"Marriage also means you *cannot* touch the thermostat without triggering a full-scale investigation. *'Who set this to 73? Are we made of money?!'* And let's be real, every married couple has the *same* fight in the car. One of you says, *'Turn here!'* The other panics, *'You didn't tell me in time!'* Now you're both lost, blaming each other, and questioning why you ever got married in the first place."

The laughter built as heads nodded across the crowd.

"They say, *'Happy wife, happy life.'* What a load of crap. My uncle says the real key to a happy marriage is knowing when to apologize. *Pro tip?* The answer is *right now.* Even if you have no idea what you did. *Especially* if you have no idea what you did."

Larry paused, shaking his head before switching gears.

"Life's tough, though. You know it's bad when you start negotiating with yourself over laundry. *'If I wear these socks inside out, I can make it one more day.'* And life? It's just one *long* game of losing things. First, it's your keys. Then it's your hairline. Eventually, it's your will to argue with the cashier."

The crowd erupted into laughter.

"And why does life always feel like a *pop quiz* you weren't prepared for? *'Surprise! Your car won't start, and your boss needs you in early!'* Life is one giant waiting game—waiting for payday, waiting for food delivery, waiting for that one person to text you back… *from 2017.*"

He sighed dramatically.

"The hardest part? Pretending to care when someone shows you pictures of their pet. *'Oh wow, your dog looks just like… every other dog I've ever seen!'*"

More laughter rolled through the room.

"And life is full of choices, sure—but they all come down to this: *Do I want to be responsible with my money, or do I want to be happy for five minutes?* Life's tough, man. And at the end of the day? *Bills, bills, bills.*"

Larry threw up his hands in mock defeat.

"Bills are like exes—they show up every month, take all your money, and leave you questioning *every* life choice that led you here. And why is it that *everything* in your house decides to break *only* when you're broke? Like, I *can't* fix my car, the sink, *and* my soul all in the same month, Universe! *Prioritize!*"

The audience roared in agreement.

"You ever have one of those weeks where the most exciting thing that happens is scoring a *'buy one, get one free'* deal at the grocery store? That's adult happiness—*free bread.* My mom used to tell me, *'Chase your dreams!'* Well, now I'm grown, and my dreams are *health insurance and a nap—a long, uninterrupted, coma-level nap.*"

Larry glanced around the crowd and grinned. "How many people here have a job?"

The entire audience raised their hands—except for Larry. A voice from the back didn't let it slide.

"Hey, Larry, why didn't you raise your hand? Don't you have a job?"

Larry smirked. "I have a *gig*, not a job. *Google the difference* so I can wrap this show up faster, will ya?"

The room exploded with laughter.

"I would *love* to have a real job one day," Larry continued, "but you know what I hate the most about jobs? Not the backstabbing coworkers, not the soul-sucking managers—no, the *job interview* itself. They always hit you with, *'What's your biggest weakness?'* And you're just sitting there, sweating, like, *'Uh... answering this question?'*"

The audience roared as he shook his head dramatically.

"And don't even get me started on the *pay*. I worked a job back in college, and man, have you ever checked your bank account and felt like it was *judging* you? *'Why did you buy*

Starbucks five times this week?' Uh, *because caffeine is cheaper than therapy, that's why!"*

He threw up his hands in mock frustration, and the audience erupted once again, completely feeling his pain.

"Bikers in the house!" Larry bellowed, motioning toward the grizzled crew in the corner. "Give it up for these *road warriors!* And look at you folks in the front row—y'all look like the rejected extras from *Sons of Anarchy.* Meanwhile, I showed up in a *Prius,* which, by the way, is parked two blocks away to protect what little dignity I have left."

He took a beat, scanning the room with a smirk. "You know what's crazy about bars like this? There's *always* that *one guy* who swears he knows the bartender personally. *'Yeah, me and Joe go way back.'* Meanwhile, Joe's behind the counter like, *'Who the hell is this guy?'"*

The audience chuckled knowingly.

"But hey, no judgment in a place like this. You could roll in wearing pajamas, and someone would still lean over and ask, *'Hey, you want a shot?'* That's the kind of hospitality I *respect.*"

He leaned on the mic stand, lowering his voice like he was about to reveal a great truth. "Speaking of shots—why do bartenders pour them like they're measuring out medicine? Like, bro, I'm not trying to cure the *plague* here, I'm just trying to *forget about my ex* for a few minutes."

The bartender whistled and pumped a fist in the air. Larry caught the gesture and shot back a thumbs-up before addressing the crowd again.

Larry grinned, holding up his hands in defense. "Alright, quick question for the fellas—fair warning, if you're married, keep your hands *down* unless you enjoy sleeping on the couch. Now, who here is familiar with a lovely woman by the name of *Lily Phillips* from OnlyFans?"

The room fell silent. Not a single hand rose.

Larry smirked. "Ladies, let this be yet another fun reminder of how *selectively* men listen. Now, let me ask this—any gentleman here willing to proudly admit they're a *two-minute man*?"

Once again, silence. Well, almost. Larry confidently raised his *own* hand, prompting a wave of laughter.

"That's fine, laugh now, cry later. For the first time in my life, I feel great about it. And here's why."

He let the anticipation build before delivering the punch.

"Lily Phillips just set a record—*101 men in 24 hours.*"

A collective groan rippled through the audience—disbelief, awe, a touch of concern.

"I know, it sounds *unreal,* but stay with me for a second. On my way here, I started running the numbers—because that's what normal people think about at a red light, right? And guess what? If every guy went back-to-back *without stopping,* each one would need to last at least *14 minutes.* Not exactly a sprint."

He leaned in, eyes twinkling with mischief. "But here's the real kicker. She's aiming *even higher* this time. *1,000 men. One day.* Now, let's circle back to that two-minute question. Not a single one of you had the confidence to raise a hand, which means, *statistically speaking,* I might be the *only* contender in this room. And since I already did the math, I can tell you this— if we're gonna hit 1,000, *every guy* has to finish in under *two minutes.* That means a room full of dudes chanting Missy Elliott's *One Minute Man* while trying to make history."

The crowd erupted, some howling, some shaking their heads in amused horror.

Larry raised his glass. "To ambition, stamina, and *questionable* life choices. Cheers!"

He walked to the nearly empty bottle of water and took another sip.

"I've never been married, but thanks to my uncle, I know *way* more about divorce than I should. His divorce hit him like a wrecking ball. His ex took half of everything—house, car, dignity. The only thing he got to keep was the *air fryer.* And even *that* had a weird rattling noise every time he turned it on."

The crowd chuckled as Larry shook his head.

"Divorce is strange, man. One minute, you're splitting bills; the next, you're negotiating custody over the *Netflix password.* My uncle told me, 'Kid, I knew it was over when she started labeling *her* leftovers in the fridge.' Nothing screams *'I'm emotionally checked out*' like a lasagna container with *Do Not Touch* written in permanent marker."

He let the laughter breathe before diving into the next round.

"And let's talk about divorce court. The judge asked my uncle what he wanted to keep, and he just sighed and said, *'Can I at least get my self-respect back?'* Judge didn't even hesitate—*'Nope. That's hers too.'* Divorce is basically a VIP membership to a club you *never* signed up for. And every guy in there has the same story—*'Yeah, she took my boat too.'*"

The audience erupted.

"But if you thought *divorce* was bad, try *dating* after divorce. That's a *war zone.* You're out there swiping through profiles, and *everyone* looks like they just survived the same emotional battlefield."

"My own breakup? Brutal. The tables and chairs you're sitting on have seen it. Hell, the bartender and the owner, Tom, could probably *testify.*"

Laughter rolled through the room.

"People told me, *'At least now you have your freedom.'* Freedom? Bro, I'm sitting alone on a Friday night, eating *instant ramen* in my boxers. This isn't *freedom*—it's *solitary confinement*. And they *love* saying, *'Time heals all wounds.'* Yeah? Well, my watch must be broken because it's been two years, and the only thing I've healed is my *high score* on Candy Crush."

The audience cackled as Larry leaned in, shaking his head.

"And dating apps? Just a bunch of people *pretending* they love hiking. Nobody loves hiking! We're all just trying to look outdoorsy while binge-watching Netflix and eating chips in bed."

"One of the *blessings* of being single? No more *in-laws*. God bless 'em, but *yuck.*"

"In-laws are the only people who say, *'Make yourself at home,'* and then give you the *death stare* the second you put your feet on the coffee table."

The audience chuckled in agreement.

"My uncle's *former* mother-in-law had *Spidey senses* for relaxation. The moment he sat down? *'So, when are you painting the guest room?'*

"You *know* you've really won over your in-laws when they start gossiping about their own family *in front of you.* That's the *ultimate* sign of acceptance."

The laughter grew as Larry shook his head.

"My ex's dad gave me marriage advice the first day I met him. Thought he was some wise old sage. He leaned in real serious and said, *'Just say, 'Yes, dear.''* I said, *'Wow, you really believe in compromise.'* He said, *'Compromise? No, survival.'*"

The crowd roared.

"After my breakup, my friend had this *brilliant* idea: *'Dude, you need to hit the gym. It'll help you physically and emotionally— you'll get ripped, boost your confidence, and women will be all over you.'*"

"The next thing I knew, he gave me a *full-year* gym membership. Generous, right? Or maybe he just wanted me *out of the house* so I'd stop whining about my ex."

The crowd chuckled knowingly.

"Now, I don't know if any of you have been to the gym lately, but those *treadmills?* They look *harmless.* Just sitting there, all quiet, like they're whispering, *'Come on, buddy. Let's take a nice little jog.'"*

Larry shook his head, eyes wide.

"That's a *lie. Treadmills are the psychopaths of gym equipment.*"

The audience leaned in, hooked.

"So, there I am, standing on the treadmill, feeling good. The belt's moving at a *grandma-approved* walking pace. I'm thinking, *'Man, this fitness thing? Easy. I could do this all day.'"*

"Then the screen flashes this button: *'RANDOM WORKOUT.'*"

"And me, being a *complete* moron, I press it."

The audience started laughing, *knowing* exactly where this was going.

"That thing *took off* like it had been waiting for this moment its *entire* life. One second, I'm strolling like I'm in a Sunday farmers' market. The next, I'm fighting for survival. The belt's *flying,* my legs are doing some sort of *uncoordinated Irish jig,* my hands are slapping every button in sight—I look like I'm *breakdancing against my will.*"

Larry flailed his arms and mimicked a panicked sprint, feet skidding wildly. The crowd *erupted.*

"And you know what's worse? It's not even the fall."

He paused, letting the anticipation build.

"It's that sound when you hit the emergency stop button. That loud, high-pitched screech that basically yells, 'EVERYBODY LOOK AT THIS IDIOT!'"

At this point, the audience lost it. People doubled over, wiping away tears, some gasping for air between fits of laughter.

"I'm lying there, face down, wheezing like I barely survived a National Geographic documentary. My body is sprawled out, my dignity nowhere to be found. And, of course, right next to me? A group of bodybuilders. Absolute mountains of muscle, flexing, grunting—looking like they eat protein powder straight from the tub. Not one of them rushes to help."

No, this guy—arms the size of my entire torso—leans down, tilts his head, and goes, "'Hey man, you good? You gotta tighten your core.'"

The audience lost it again. Some pounded their tables, others clutched their stomachs from laughing so hard.

Larry threw up his hands in exaggerated defeat.

"So yeah, no more treadmills for me. I've retired. Now, I just jog outside—where the only thing that can kill me is traffic."

The room erupted into applause, whistles cutting through the laughter. Larry stepped back from the mic, grinning. Another night, another crowd falling victim to *The Treadmill Joke.* This one was a keeper.

He stood center stage, microphone in hand, letting the laughter ripple through the bar like an aftershock. Scanning the room, he took in the bikers clinking their beers, a cop nodding in amusement, a guy in a poncho waving like they were old friends, and a couple in matching denim flashing him a thumbs-up. The energy was electric. For a moment, Larry felt like he was floating.

"You know, when I walked in tonight, I wasn't sure how this would go. I see bikers, cops, a guy in a MAGA hat, my Black brothers, and, of course, Poncho Guy over there… This could've gone a lot of different ways."

The crowd cheered, hooting in agreement.

"But man, you all? You've been nothing but amazing."

The applause grew louder, a few whistles echoing from the back.

"Comedy's a weird thing. It's about taking what makes us different and laughing about it together. And tonight? I think we nailed it. We poked fun at the cop who gave me a speeding ticket, celebrated the unmatched hustle of my Mexican brothers, and even found common ground with the MAGA guy—mostly because we *all* agree that Netflix needs to fix their damn password system."

The room exploded. Laughter, applause, claps on the bar, people doubling over. Larry took a slow step back, soaking it all in.

"Alright, everyone, I can't overlook today's trending topic. Ladies and gentlemen, it finally happened—TikTok went dark in America. The government took one look at the endless dance challenges, chaotic trends, and an army of teenagers declaring themselves 'influencers' and said, 'Enough.'"

He paused.

"Suddenly, Americans were in crisis mode. *'Where will we express ourselves?! Where will we post our deep, meaningful thoughts on life?!'*" Larry clutched his chest in dramatic despair before lowering his voice to a whisper.

"Then, from the shadows, one voice said, *'I hear there's an app from China…'*"

He let the moment sink in.

"And just like that, America—self-proclaimed champion of free speech—collectively sprinted toward a Chinese app in search of freedom. The irony here? So thick, you could spread it on toast."

The crowd roared, and Larry let the laughter simmer before continuing.

"You'd think banning TikTok would make us more productive, right? Wrong. Instead, Americans—being the relentlessly resourceful people we are—discovered a new obsession: an app called *RedNote*."

He shook his head.

"Here's the crazy part. RedNote has been around for years, but no one in America cared. Then suddenly, TikTok disappears, and *boom!* We 'discover' RedNote like we're Christopher Columbus pulling up to an already occupied island. I swear, at this rate, we're gonna plant a flag in it and declare, *'We discovered RedNote!'*"

The audience howled with laughter.

"RedNote is basically digital Ellis Island at this point. But instead of a Statue of Liberty, there's a giant neon sign flashing: *'Send us your influencers, your lip-syncers, your thirst-trappers yearning for viral fame.'* And you know what Americans did? We lined up like it was Black Friday at Walmart. Because let's be real—we don't care who's watching, as long as we can post ourselves dancing badly on the internet."

The audience erupted again, some wiping away tears from laughing so hard.

"And then you've got the TikTok refugees—wandering through the digital wilderness, desperately trying to rebuild their clout. They set up camp on Instagram, trying to make Reels happen. But let's be honest—Instagram is like that one uncle who tries *way* too hard to be cool and just ends up embarrassing himself."

Larry paused for dramatic effect.

"And then there's *YouTube Shorts.*"

A few audience members groaned in anticipation.

"Oh yeah, you know what I'm talking about. YouTube Shorts is like TikTok's awkward cousin—always showing up late to the party, copying everyone's dance moves, and just standing there hoping someone will notice them."

The crowd lost it.

Larry grinned, stepping back, basking in the laughter.

"The TikTok refugees were out there, desperately rebuilding their followings—one cringy duet at a time. It was like watching a group of influencers wander through a digital wasteland, clinging to their ring lights for warmth."

"And me? I was just sitting back, popcorn in hand, thinking, *This is the most American thing I have ever witnessed.*"

Larry shook his head, still grinning.

"America—the land of free speech—decided to ban an app because, well… too much free speech. Suddenly, people who hadn't read the Constitution since high school were out here screaming, *'You can take my rights, but don't you dare take my 15-second dance clips!'*"

The audience burst into laughter, a few people clapping in agreement.

"And the real kicker? Here we are, getting our First Amendment fix from the same country that censors Winnie the Pooh. Folks, I swear, some days satire just writes itself."

Larry let the laughter breathe before dropping the next punchline.

"And speaking of irony—let's talk about Donald Trump for a second. Half the country thought he was against free speech, right? And yet, suddenly, here he comes, riding in like a digital savior, promising to bring back TikTok."

He leaned into the mic, his voice dripping with mock disbelief.

"Imagine a firefighter who *hates* water. Spends years yelling, *'Water is dangerous! Ban it! It's causing more harm than good!'* He insists that fires can be handled his way—with sand, controlled burns, whatever."

"Then, one day, wildfires are raging, people are begging for water, and this guy suddenly announces, *'You know what? I've always been pro-water. I love water. I'm gonna bring it back for every home and every hydrant!"*

The audience roared.

"That's exactly how I felt watching Trump promise to restore TikTok. After years of blasting social media for being biased or harmful, now he's all in for an app that's basically the Wild West of free expression?"

Larry shook his head, still grinning.

"I never thought I'd say this, but... *Thank you, President Trump, for defending our right to behave badly online.*"

The room erupted. Laughter, cheers, and more than a few people raising their drinks in approval. Larry stepped back, smirking—another night, another crowd loving the chaos.

"Honestly, nights like this remind me exactly why I do this. To share a laugh. To connect. To prove that no matter where we come from, what we believe, or how utterly ridiculous our lives get—we all have something to smile about."

He let the moment settle, scanning the room.

"So, thank you. Thank you for showing up. Thank you for laughing—even at the jokes that really didn't deserve it. And thank you for giving me a reason to keep chasing this wild, wonderful, completely insane dream of mine."

The room erupted. Applause thundered through the walls, whistles and cheers bouncing off the ceiling. Larry grinned, soaking it in, then gave a small, theatrical bow.

"I'm Larry, and I'll see you again sometime—hopefully not in Officer O'Malley's rearview mirror. *Goodnight!*"

With one last wave, Larry stepped off the stage, the applause still ringing in his ears. For the first time, he didn't just *hope* he was a comedian.

He *felt* like one.

And he couldn't wait to do it all over again.

TO BE CONTINUED...

www.ingramcontent.com/pod-product-compliance
Ingram Content Group UK Ltd.
Pitfield, Milton Keynes, MK11 3LW, UK
UKHW040724270325
456784UK00006B/38